I0622007

In Poe's Shadow

A collection inspired by the works of Edgar Allan Poe

Edited by

A. W. Gifford &
Jennifer L. Gifford

Dark Opus Press
P.O. Box 1013
Gayson, Ga 30017

www.betenoiremagazine.com

In Poe's Shadow is published by Dark Opus Press a division of Charm Noir Omnimedia P.O Box 1013, Grayson, Ga 30017

ISBN-13: 978-0615537528
ISBN-10: 0615537529

Contents

Introduction

"Beauty of whatever kind, in its supreme development, invariably excites the sensitive soul to tears." - Edgar Allan Poe

Though his life only spanned forty years, Edgar Allen Poe managed to fashion a name for himself in both American and World Literature. Much of the facts of Poe's life have been slanderized and romanticed, heeding to largely speculated interpretations about his character. A dope addict, manic-depressive, epileptic, alcoholic—all Freudianized explanations for his literary genius.

Further speculation hints to Poe's tumultuous childhood. Both of Poe's parents were actors, and many biographers suggest Poe's flare for the dramatic came from his family's profession. Yet his childhood was marked by infinite sadness. His father, though an accomplished actor, was a more accomplished alcoholic. He abandoned the family when Edgar was a year old. The following year, Poe's mother died. The children were adopted out, with young Edgar being taken in as a foster child by John Allen. Hard living, misfortune, and bad luck shadowed Poe through his adulthood and some of those misfortunes manifested themselves in Poe's earlier works like *The Fall of the House of Usher* and *William Wilson*.

Few writers create outside their current time and setting, and he was no exception. Poe stands out amongst his contemporaries as one of the leading authors of the Romantic era, yet he was a complex writer whose style isn't easy to articulate. While Poe's style followed most of the literary elements notorious of his peers, his style clearly leaned toward the gothic. But where other writers tried to define the comprehensive socio-political views of the Romantic era, Poe took his writing a step further.

Edgar Allen Poe wanted his literary works final effects to strike emotion in his readers.

Often Poe created an immediate sense of kinship with reader because his intangible characters were given a three dimensional feel to them, making them instantly relatable. Throughout his works, his characters — M. Dupin in *Murders in the Rue Morgue* or Roderick Usher in *The Fall of the House of Usher* — are clear examples of Poe creating characters dominated by emotions, which explain for the often chaotic and sometimes illogical behavior of the characters. Poe often reasoned that his characters were more lifelike because they mirrored man; and men often sense and feel things long before they contemplate them.

Poe created settings in far off and non-existent places in order to allow the reader to delve themselves wholly into the atmospheric symbolism which is the sole emphasis of Poe's story. His lack of complete names for his characters is done purposefully. This allows the reader to experience the emotions of Poe's characters without succumbing to eccentricities of a character's identity. It doesn't matter that we don't know the name of the narrator in *The Pit and the Pendulum*. What's important is that as readers, we identify with him in sensing his fear and terror stricken reactions.

To summarize Poe presents an improbability. His literary genius spanned poetry, short stories, novellas, and critical essays. Whatever the role, Poe's works have been a source of pleasure and entertainment for scholars and readers alike. More the century after his death, his works continue to inspire new writers and ensnare new readers. His classic tales of gothic literature continue to strike a chord in the hearts and imagination of countless Poe enthusiasts all over the world.

—Jennifer L. Gifford
September, 2011

The Resurrectionist

Existence precedes essence. The earth overflows with embryonic possibilities, of heroes and villains, of strength and frailty, of life and its manifold miseries. How is it that ere my birth, fate determined that I be ill-favored and ill-framed? That I be the last in a line of once revered and honored giants, given to a handful of parasites subsisting on the residue of a glorious past. But, as in nature, day follows night; evil succeeds good and death flows from life.

My Christian name is Erasmus; of my family surname I shall not speak. My lineage cannot be traced. No crypt bears the family crest nor graves mark our passing. No shaded plot exists where mourners go to place a wreath and touch dry lip to cold stone. None speak of us in the public square, save in the hushed tones of backhand discourse. My forebears carried pick and spade, our ancestral home smelled of earth, and the family tub displayed the concentric strata of an archeological dig.

My earliest memories were of that tub. Therein was I born, and there my mother died. In scarlet waters I emerged with the assistance of a drunken aunt. That selfsame fluid bore the infection that would send my mother sweating to an early death and leave me a sickly infant of indeterminate longevity. With spidery limbs and shallow breath, of doughy complexion and weak eyes, I lingered through infancy.

Auntie nursed me with some reluctance, sparing what little maternity she possessed for her own daughter, Martine. Auntie's aversion manifested itself in abandoning me to my own devices and sending Martine away to boarding school at the earliest. My only contact with my sweet cousin was her infrequent visits during holidays. From her alabaster hand I learned to read and to write. She'd leave her old school books behind for me to wrestle knowledge from. Had I not been misshapen and unworthy, I would have been betrothed to Martine. But Auntie broke tradition and desired nothing more than her child cut the familial bonds.

Auntie would shepherd me to the bath where her sister died, point to the black bloodstains soaked into the grout and recount my birth in inebriated mutterings. With a firm hand she'd press my face to the cool tiles and curse the day I took her beloved from her bosom. Despite her ravings and madness, I clung to Auntie constantly. For when she was not in her cups, she could be kind and often gave me a tincture of opium before bed. Many a night I left my frail form below and wandered through the ethereal planes. When my spirited wanderings became a terror, I'd find solace within the bath.

In that bath I spent my youth, scrubbing the tub, the terrazzo, the tile. I used an old toothbrush and a thousand capfuls of bleach to whiten the grout, to clean the claws on the tub, to scrub until my mind reeled from the vapors. The bath became my oasis in a foul world, my retreat from the feculence of life. Some hours after midnight, Father and Uncles would return to invade my sanctuary. Muddy boots rolled like obsidian stones across the white tiles. Flea-infested coats and coveralls spread a pestilence of vermin that hid beneath the tub and in every crevice of the bath. When Father and Uncles had washed and despoiled my ceramic altar, my enameled basin, they moved on to the dining room. I returned with brush and bucket to bend to my labor.

Once done, I would retreat to my bedchamber down a passageway filled with dancing motes and daunting cobwebs. Wool curtains kept the manor in eternal twilight. Copper pipes brought a yellowed gaslight that threatened to set ablaze the peeling wallpaper. Frames hung askew, devoid of portraits as a constant reminder of pasts forgotten and the certainty of my demise.

When eldest Uncle died from smallpox, Father found me, as was my wont, in the bath removing ages of soot from the windowsill, scrubbing the embedded rings of dirt from the tub and erasing the signs of my mother's death from the tile. Having survived twelve winters, he accepted my existence as his progeny and took pains to bring me into the family trade. Taking away my brush, he led me out to a waiting wagon. Younger Uncle held the reigns from atop his perch whilst the eldest lay wrapped in sacking amid two spades.

The moon rode high as our cart trundled beneath it, into a small graveyard no larger than a common garden. A freshly filled grave lay before us with a spray of wilting flowers on the loosened earth. Father handed me a spade.

"Dig." He ordered. I grasped the blade in my bleached hands and took up the family trade.

Hands blistered and joints aching, I dug as Father commanded whilst Uncle lectured on the various methods of unearthing a grave. In an hour, with muscles spent and sinews worn to the breaking point, I struck the coffin lid. Uncle replaced me allowing me some respite. I rolled onto the wet grass and watched the stars swim across the heavens. Short of breath and vision spotted, my spirit desired nothing more than to join those bodies high in the ether.

Replacing the fresh corpse with Uncle, we ended the night with a few gentle words over his resting place and filled the grave. I had hitherto suspected what my elders did on their nightly endeavors, having seen and cleaned up after their rounds as well as spying their boastings over what booty could be claimed from the dead. The act of desecration left me empty as the tombs they robbed and my soul yearning for release.

The vulgar, the simple, the common, call us grave robbers. Amongst my kin and our clientele we are known as resurrection men. For by us, the dead rise to find a higher purpose. A base laborer whose life yielded naught but misery and pain can, in death, educate surgeons to better ply their trade. None would dare to purchase a body riddled with contagion, else Uncle would have been sold, as my mother had been. By the morn, I could not recall where Eldest Uncle lay. A ghoulish calling is the resurrectionist and t'was my heritage, my duty.

I spent my nights crawling down holes only wide enough to draw out the corpse. Uncle dug the pit and broke through the casket with his spade while Father kept watch. The muffled crack of the casket lid signaled my part in the macabre play was at hand. On my belly I crawled into the void. Father and Uncle holding me by the ankles like Thetis dipping Achilles in the Styx.

Night after night I returned to the earth that spat out the first man. Into Sheol, into darkness, into the heart of death I ventured. Soil rained down in my eyes and filled my nose with the cloying scent of decay. Root tendrils pulled at me, snatching my coat, catching my trousers, beckoning me to stay. I descended until I came nose to nose with necrosis and drew a rope behind the body and under the arms. Slowly, steadily, Uncle and Father would draw us out enjoined to ensure the corpse not cling to the casket. Cheek to jowl, I embraced the Grim Reaper night after endless night.

When the work became unbearable and the pit called with its stygian darkness, I cringed at the prospect of taking the dead by the hand. While my body did the work, my spirit rose to notions of courage, of honor, of Martine; as my hands grappled with cold flesh, my vision ascended to hover above. Those visions lasted only a moment and would come without benefit of the opiate. I once overheard Uncle speaking to Father about this whilst I hung deep in the grave. My sight may have been weak but my hearing was keen.

"Think it wise brother, to use Erasmus so?" Uncle questioned Father.

"The lad needed to know, and we needed a third."

"Not that, it's the boy's condition, I mean to say. He's feeble. Can barely tie a decent knot, and can dig not at all." I heard concern in Uncle's voice.

"The work will strengthen him, as it did us when we were lads."

"To be sure, brother. But what of his spirit? It's as feeble as his body. It slips off him like our gloves. One day it will depart and not return."

"Then we will have two bodies to sell. Enough talk. Lift the lad out now."

When at last our labor was done and gold crossed palms, we'd sally home, shed our ghastly attire and bathe. Only when all had left and my sanctuary properly defiled with the dregs of the graveyard, I'd retrieve the jug of chlorinated bleach from my bedchamber and set out to make all things new again.

The only light in my wretchedness came from the countenance of my cousin Martine. In summer and on holidays she would return from her New England boarding school and take pity on me. During those respites, the family refrained from its grisly commerce and for a time normalcy reigned. Doors thrown open, light and air entered my world. A furious cleaning preceded her visits making those the most joyful times of the year.

Sweet Martine. From her rosy lips I heard music and laughter. In her blue eyes I found both hope and charity. Her smile bewitched me and her teeth, straight as a razor with no stain or sign of decay, held me enraptured. Those teeth, as white as the ceramic tile that bordered the bath, allowed me to forget my misery. For a time, I put my brush and bleach aside to bask in her lambency. She became my sun, my splendor each day she remained.

The only visitors to the manor came when Martine resided there. When children, her classmates came by for tea and cakes. When we grew older and her beauty could not be hid behind woolen drapes, suitors buzzed about like bottle flies. At those times I no longer dreaded my spade nor the hungry earth. I saw the grave as that part of nature that removes the unwanted, the puerile, to stow them beneath the rich loam never to be seen again. I watched those boys with the cold knowledge of a thousand empty graves longing to be filled. And though jealousy grew in my heart, I could no further blame the besotted callers than I could my own desire for Martine.

Many a night I looked down from my bedchamber window to fuzzy-faced devotees cast adrift in her eyes. They held her hand as I never could and received the softness of her kiss upon their cheeks as I only dreamed. Save for one event that I dismissed as a waking dream, a most delusional chimera.

I was by happenstance, beneath the porch with a sack of boric acid to kill the vermin therein, when Martine and admirer alighted upon it after a long walk. I glimpsed through the chinks in the wood, my cousin's face and the light of the setting sun in her eyes. How at that moment I wished most ardently to be another, to be anyone but myself and free to adore her. What empty words her adherent said I could not tell. He reached into his waistcoat for a pocket watch and the light of the sun flashed off its silver surface blinding me for a moment.

I blinked and to my astonishment I stood before Martine, looking at her through the clear eyes of another, holding her delicate fingers with the strange grip of a healthy hand. My mouth moved but the words seemed muted, muffled as though speaking through a long pipe. What transcendentalism I experienced, I cannot say. What ecstatic mysticism took hold of my spirit and placed it in this stranger's mind I could not begin to fathom. It mattered not, for the look in Martine's eyes was enough. As was the closeness of her lips until, at last, they pressed upon his, upon mine. I opened my eyes and beheld the two lovers break the kiss from my vantage beneath the porch.

Surely it was a fancy, a mere delusion brought on by the multitude of vapors ingested in my nightly ablutions. Try as I might to castigate the memory, I could never obliterate the sweetness of her lips from my mind.

Like quicksilver the days slipped by and Martine abandoned me once again. For weeks after her visits I could find no consolation save the whiteness of tub, the terrazzo, the tile. Their cool surfaces assuaged my brow and gave succor to my torment. On the eve of her departure, the doors closed and the light shut out. I'd yearn for my brush only to grasp a spade. Duty called, and as youth waxed to manhood, I accepted my place in the world. I adopted a cold heart, a temperament of ice, a desultory desire and excelled at the art of resurrection.

I grew in strength, transforming the base act of grave robbery to an art. No longer did we burrow into graves like beasts, and drag corpses from their resting places covered in filth. I adopted methods of careful excavation and respectful exhumation, often leaving the grave in a better condition than when I found it. Possessions remained in the unbroken coffins, I could not abide thievery. The bodies, I brought home and washed until they were as pure a form as I could provide. Wrapped in white shrouds, I presented the bodies in such a manner as to leave my patrons speechless.

With each passing season the angel of death called my kin and they answered. Uncle hailed to consumption, Aunty to cirrhosis and Father to diabetes. In the space of a year I went from servant to master of the manor. As each fell, I buried them in the graves of strangers. Except for Auntie, whose physique was of such excellent condition, with no sign of disease or morbidity. She fetched a goodly sum.

What does a slave know of freedom when it is laid at his feet? Does he not give a backward glance to the plow and yearn, imperceptibly, for the lash? So too did I cast myself into labors both day and night. From the necropolis I freed the shells of the departed and within my own home I broke the shackles binding my desires.

I sent word to Martine, words of love, words of matrimony. I opened my heart to her and begged her return at the soonest. I confess, with my failing eyes, my own words smeared across the sheet in a jungle of lines. I trusted to the singularity of Martine's character to know the meaning of my letter.

Until her response I endeavored to rid the manor of the stench of neglect. With every layer of grime removed from my home I felt the weight of my ancestors' sins roll off my shoulders. With bleach and lye, muriatic acid and ammonia, chlorinated mercury and whitewash I attacked each room, each hall, each square inch of space.

I pulled down the wool curtains and ripped each clinging shred of wallpaper that I could perceive. I scrubbed the walls with a wire brush until plaster dust coated me. The carpets, wall hangings, anywhere filth could lurk was cast out, burned in a pyre and the ashes buried. Buried in the black humus that eventually consumes all. A sort of monomania came over me where I found corruption in every corner. I could not rest until my home was clean, until I was clean.

Donning gloves and mask, I ripped the floorboards out and scrubbed the wood top and bottom until it was as white as my own skin. What could not be cleaned to an acceptable level of purity was doused in a generous coating of whitewash. In each room I left a stage of clean devastation, oft leaving nothing but the supporting beams until the interior of the manor took on the appearance of a Greek ruin lost in the empty arctic. Where once darkness ruled, my manor became a palace of light.

The compulsions did not end at the manor but incorporated my own flesh. My hair I shaved to give lice no refuge and my nails I kept trimmed to precisely one eighth of an inch. No foods could I eat that were not of the purest color and quality. For a wardrobe, I donned highly starched fabric of pure cotton, blanched straw hats and white patent leather boots.

When, at last, my delirium ebbed and I discovered my home sufficiently purified, I took note of several correspondence beneath the letterbox. The letters were splattered with bleach and whitewash and dates going back more than a month. My passion had possessed me for more than a fortnight and I had no knowledge of time passing.

Her neat script, washed away to near transparency, save for a few fragments, a word or two survived. All were addressed to Auntie. Surely, I told her of her mother's demise. The few words discernable, 'consented', 'bride', and 'arrive soonest'. What rapture took my heart, what joy. Soon my beloved Martine and I would be one.

Within a week she arrived in a burst of color and perfume. Throwing open the door, she called out. "Mama!"

I stepped into the vestibule and noticed with growing dread my cousin was not well. Her once perfect skin was now sun-scorched to an unhealthy chestnut color; her hollow cheeks were puffy and full. Most frightfully, the look in her eyes as she crossed the threshold of our ancestral home told me all I needed to know. My dear cousin had gone mad.

Had I the ability to shed tears, before the fumes of my sanitations rid me of them, I would most assuredly have wept. Hands shaking in a palsy, trembling mouth unable to utter a word, her eyes, blue as lake ice, grew wide, grew wild until a paroxysm overtook her and she collapsed at my feet.

Martine, sweet Martine, the vile world had contaminated her perfection. I gathered her up and took her to the only place that could rid her of the worldly stain. To the bath.

I laid her in the tub as I would a babe in its crib. I considered calling on a physician but dismissed the thought immediately. I knew the cause of her malady. Her humors had fallen out of balance from multifarious diseases. The infestations of the unwashed rabble had entered through the pores, clogging them. The only treatment for such a condition was purification. It was left up to me to cleanse her, to wash all the impurities away.

Out came the sodium phosphate, the muriatic acid, the bleach. I laid the instruments of my passion upon a cloth by the tub. A steel pick that roots out filth from any crevice, a long handled grater that removes the most stubborn rot and an array of gleaming steel brushes of varying sizes. Soon my sweet cousin would be as pure and clean as the tub.

Deftly and respectfully, I removed only enough of Martine's clothing as deemed proper and befitting a young woman of her station. I slipped on my mask and rubber gloves and grasped the steel pick when the sounds of a commotion stayed my hand. Shouts came from the vestibule, a man's voice.

"Martine, Martine!" he called in ever-increasing timbre.

What whims of providence made this invader, this interloper enter my home at that moment, and what had he to do with my sweet Martine? I noticed at that moment, a ring upon her left hand, a wedding ring. Footfalls echoed in the corridor approaching fast.

The door to the bath burst open. A young man, dark of hair with a swarthy complexion held the door handle in one hand and a silver-capped cane in the other. His eyes darted from Martine, disrobed in the tub to the steel spike in my hand and the gallons of acid lined neatly before the tub.

A look of unrestrained rage contorted his features. Up went the cane, ready to rain down death. Time slowed its relentless pace. I stepped outside the temporal plane and saw with perfect clarity the events play out in the most miniscule increments.

I held the elongated pick in a manner to defend myself. The man, nay Martine's husband, for I took notice of the matching band on his finger, approached with mouth agape and frenzy in his eyes. Raising my arm several degrees, I held the pick like a rapier.

I could see, in my mind's eye, the pick going into his open mouth and penetrating the soft flesh of his upper palate. His momentum would drive the steel deep into his brain and snuff the light out of his eyes as easily as blowing out a candle.

My arm straightened, ready to dispatch Martine's husband, when in the periphery of my vision I saw, in the reflection of a silver-framed mirror, an image more terrible than any I could ever conceive.

I beheld a hero and a villain, one hale and handsome, the other sickly and soulless. Even through my weakened eyes I saw my masked visage, the red-rimmed eyes, unblinking as a lizard and the paper-thin skin stretched across the skull like dried parchment. Feckless fate, cruel Moira to cast me in so low a role. Only by fortuitous chance that I was not the husband rushing through the door, that I was the vile creature to be destroyed.

Only a moment had passed, only the blinking of an eye. Clarity burned through the fog of my madness, truth assailed me at the moment of my death. I knew what needed be done. Relaxing my arm, I loosened the grip on the spike. Death was preferable to an existence in such pure and spotless evil. Ere my end, I gave up my spirit; left my body and felt the life fade from my body before the cane cleaved my skull.

I saw my body fall, saw the blood flow over the tiles and seep into the grout. My vision was impeccable and crisp, I breathed unimpeded with no asthmatic wheezing. I felt strength in my bones, strength through my very being. I looked at my hands; turned the cane see the bloodstained silver cap.

I stepped to the mirror and touched a foreign face, the face of Martine's husband. His name was John, and I know with certainty that by some transcendentalism I had been given a second chance, a new life. Where John went, his spirit, his being, I hadn't the least notion. Perhaps he resided within, a prisoner in his own body. I had his memories, his skills, and for Martine I possessed the love of two lives, two hearts.

A year has passed since that fateful day. Martine doesn't wish to speak of it and utters not a word of her past. Though I believe she suspects something is amiss, particularly on those evenings where she finds me in the bath, with a brush, with the bleach.

She never wanted to return to the manor. But John could ill-afford such a grand place, and it was presently vacant. She rarely ventures to the lower level where I conduct my trade. John's medical training has enabled me to begin a new venture as well as continue the family tradition. By day, I am John Maynard, mortician and embalmer, well respected and highly praised pillar of the community.

By night, when the stars traverse the ether, I don my white and pick up my spade. I am Erasmus, the resurrectionist. I sell the dead.

✠

AP Diggs *lives in Michigan and works for a major airline. He has had a previous story published on* Apollo's Lyre *(June 2010). He is married with a teenage son, loves gardening and has a weakness for zombie movies. A member of the Flash Factory and a co-administrator in a writer's group. This is his second publication.*

Merryl

James S. Dorr

He dreamed he had cut the tip of his finger off. He did not know how, or else he had forgotten by the time he woke up. But the image stayed with him, his middle fingertip down to just above the first knuckle.

This was the finger that Merryl, his ex-girlfriend, used to suck when they started to make love. It was the one she called her "pleasure finger."

He wanted — he longed — to forget about Merryl. She had cursed him when she left for good that rainy afternoon, claiming as always that it was *his* fault, of course. After they had had one too many arguments. She'd slapped his face, screaming, "You're going to regret this. The rest of your life, Johnny!" Merryl had always been one for dramatics.

He tried to defend himself, but she just shrieked louder. "I've had it Johnny. You're such a bastard — just thinking of yourself. You and those slob friends of yours. Just wait and see, you'll always remember now. How good you had it once. How good *I* was for you!"

He had laughed at her — then.

But the next morning he read in the newspaper about the accident, how, seething with anger, she had driven too fast when she left his apartment and skidded on the turnoff to the highway. She was dead before they got her to the hospital.

He had zombie-walked through the funeral. He owed that to her parents who didn't know that they had broken up. None of which helped him to forget her like he wanted, to just get on with his life like it had been before he met her.

To find someone new.

But now this *dream*, this was something else again. Okay, he hadn't really slept well in the month since the funeral either. He even went to the doctor about it, at the factory where he worked. The doctor told him, "It's normal enough, John. When something like that happens, it's only natural that you'll have some feelings of guilt, even though none of it was really your fault. Sure, she was upset at you, but what you need to concentrate on is that it was she who made the decision to drive too fast. So, just try to accept it."

He thanked the doctor. Yeah, *try* to accept it!

And now this dream — well, he wasn't going to go to the doctor again about *this*. At least it took his mind off Merryl, especially when he had it again the following night. Once again his finger had been cut off, just the tip with the nail to the top of the first knuckle. But the thing was, and now he remembered that it had been a part of the first dream too, there hadn't been any pain. Rather a sort of bemused curiosity as he picked the finger tip up and gazed at it. There hadn't been blood to speak of either, but just a sort of soft yet firm feel to it as he rolled it between the thumb and first finger of his other hand, holding it up to peer at it more closely.

He held it in front of his mouth — *and he ate it.*

He woke up, shaking. *That* was what he had dreamed before too. Now he remembered. And one more thing as well, that he could not recall what it had tasted like — even if it had had any taste at all — but he could remember in detail how it had *felt* in his mouth when he chewed it. He thought of the crunch, the splitting of the nail, but even more he remembered, exactly, the texture of the flesh. Rubbery, sort of, like seafood he'd had once, at some kind of exotic Eastern restaurant that Merryl had insisted they go to.

He remembered having been vaguely sick then — but now the texture fascinated him. What restaurant had it been? What kind of seafood? Octopus maybe? Some kind of squid? Something that men like him normally would not have chosen to eat themselves.

Something closely packed and white — "Hold it now, Johnny," he said to himself. "This is starting to go too far."

He brushed his teeth three times, not so much to get the flavor out — because he still did not recall whether, in his dream, it had even *had* flavor — but rather as a sort of symbolic prophylactic to guard, he hoped, against any such memory returning to bother him later.

He finally got to work late that morning. He went directly to his machine, running it fast to make up for lost time.

Just before lunch, the tip of his finger was caught by the blade!

He powered down instantly, as he had been trained to. The man at the station next to his hit the button to call for help.

There didn't seem to be that much bleeding, at least not like what he might have expected—he thought of his dream!—nor very much pain either. "Shock," the company doctor said. "Here, let me spray this on. It's an anesthetic as well as a disinfectant. You fainted for a moment there, John, which may have been just as well. I ended up having to put a few stitches in. Now let me put a bandage on it too, just to keep the dirt away from it."

The doctor droned on. He thought he might have fainted again, the next thing he remembered being handed a paper to sign.

"It's an agreement," the doctor said. "We had hoped to sew the cut part back on, but no one could find it on the floor around your machine, so all this says is that you acknowledge that we did our best. We're going to give you two weeks off—still being paid, mind you—to give yourself a chance to recover. Then, once you come back in and get the stitches out, well, your middle finger *will* be shorter, but it needn't cause you any problems. Fortunately, it was on your left hand."

Then later, at home, when he reached with his right hand into his pants pocket, he found the finger there.

He put it in the refrigerator—he wasn't quite sure why. It was too late to call the doctor, to have it sewn back *now*. The doctor had explained about that, about how it would have had to have been done right away, before there could even be the slightest damage from rotting.

Perhaps he would give it a burial later. It didn't seem right, somehow, to just throw it away in the garbage.

Then he remembered the flavor, not in his dream, but of the octopus, whatever it had been, that he had eaten in the restaurant with Merryl. It had been bland, not fishy at all, but with some kind of slight *sweet* aftertaste to it.

He thought he would be ill.

He opened a beer and turned on the TV, placing a pack of cigarettes —another of Merryl's and his disagreements—on the table beside his chair. He skipped having dinner. By the time the cigarette pack was half empty, he called it a night and went to bed early.

He dreamed of the finger, this time concentrating on his curiosity as he inspected the tip from every side, holding it up in front of his face. He inspected the nail, the whorls of the print when he turned it around, the way the flesh yielded when his fingers pressed it. The fragile elasticity of its skin.

Before popping it in his mouth.

He woke up sweating. He felt weak, still sleepy. The doctor had told him it might take some time to adjust to the trauma, that while his accident had not been serious — not in the sense of, for instance, Merryl's death — still it, too, involved a permanent loss. It would be something he'd have to get used to.

Things might seem strange at first.

He shrugged off the feeling. He showered, carefully, making sure not to get the bandage on his left hand wet. He shaved and brushed his teeth.

In the kitchen he reached in the icebox for milk for his cereal. There on the middle shelf he saw the fingertip, resting on a small plate wrapped in clear plastic film, just as he had left it.

He felt, as in his dream, curiosity wash over him in waves. Not resisting, he reached with his right hand to take the plate out, to peel the wrap off it.

Trembling, he held it up, looking it over from every side, noting its whiteness. Its slightly wrinkled look, just like a —

He couldn't help himself, the image flooded across his mind. *Just like a penis, the whole finger that is, if he imagined the rest of the finger, soft and white, attached back onto its tip. Just like his penis after he had made love. . . .*

Everything seemed black.

The next thing he knew, he felt the texture, spongy yet firm, the crinkle of hardness of the nail against his teeth. He spat it out into the palm of his right hand. He looked at it there, flaccid, moist with spittle.

*He wondered how Merryl felt, what it was like inside her mouth when she took in his — *

Shaking, he dropped the finger back on the plate. He plunged his head under the kitchen sink faucet, turning the water on cold and hard. He couldn't help it, the bandage got wet too.

He dried his hand off as best he could. He tried to read later, in front of the TV. He forced himself to eat something for lunch, a sandwich of some kind he'd slapped together. He saw, on the kitchen table, the plate. The fingertip on the plate.

He resumed his station on the couch in front of the TV. He must have dozed off.

The next thing he knew he was back in the kitchen. He saw by the clock it was time for dinner — then felt, in his mouth, that he was already eating. A firm, yet yielding substance which, all of a sudden, flooded his mouth with a faintly sweet flavor, of meat perhaps only just turning putrescent. A short, crunchy twig of bone.

He didn't need to look at the empty plate on the table to realize what it was.

He tried to spit it out again, but this time he couldn't. It was too interesting how his teeth ground it up, shredding its last bits. How had it been when he'd first started chewing?

He'd missed that part, hadn't he?

Hungrily—no, more with curiosity, he wasn't sure which was the more intense feeling—he looked at his left hand's remaining fingers. Swallowing what was left in his mouth, without thinking, he started to unwind the bandage that swathed his middle finger's stump.

Reaching with his teeth to the stitches.

"*No!*" he shouted.

He rewrapped his wounded finger, clumsily, putting a rubber band around the bandage to hold it. He reached for a beer, a six pack of beers, to keep himself busy before he did something even more stupid. Just for a moment he thought he ought to call the doctor, but realized, of course, it was after hours. The doctor would not be there.

It did not occur to him until afterwards that he might have looked up the doctor's home phone number. By then, though, it was far too late. He drank purposely to knock himself out, to get through the night without dreaming at all—or at least not remembering—but somehow, whether awake or asleep, he saw himself taking the bandage off once more. He saw the next joint, white and flaccid looking.

He felt the springiness, once more, of severed flesh. This time a bit thicker, more satisfying.

He looked at his hand again and saw that the thumb now was missing.

Times alternated of blackness and light, of sleeping and wakefulness. He thought of what an addict's life might be like—he had once seen a movie depicting heroin addicts, living in fogs between obtaining fixes—and felt his was like that too. His was a *texture* life, feeling broad muscles against his tongue, or mouth-melting fat, or once again the celery-stalk feel of teeth crunching bone. It was all in a fog, he did not know for sure which feeling was which. Or whether he felt pain.

Just a slight, sweet flavor.

But then he knew something else. He was not *just* devouring his substance. He had wondered about that, if he was getting smaller and smaller, his body, that is, from the fingertips to the toes. Then eating inward from there to the middle. Until he reached—what? His mouth?

Could his mouth eat his mouth?

Or was there something else *that was his center. The last to be eaten.*

Or....

But it was not that, not just a diminishing, because what he ate would have to go somewhere. He first felt the tingling—he thought, in his dream, he was eating his left hip, but in his dream also he felt a growth on his chest. In his elbows, his fingers, he felt tinglings, now he remembered, had felt them already.

Darkness, lightness, wakefulness, dreams again. He had lost track of which was which, only that somehow, *something* was happening. A regeneration. A rebirth. A regrowing.

Limbs, body becoming—

What?

He thought of movies he used to like on TV, another thing Merryl had fought with him about. Had tried to change in him. Movies about people becoming insects. Insects growing large. Other animals, giant rats, spiders, even a giant ape.

So now he imagined different creatures too, like squid and octopuses. Beings that no longer had need of fingers.

Or used them differently.

What *he* was turning to—?

He thought in his dreams of misshapen behemoths—he could not see when it was dark, of course, but he could feel the weight of flesh hanging on his body differently. That his very form had changed itself somehow. In some unknown manner. That even the ends of the nerves that branched through him responded in different ways—

Then, at last, he woke up.

What little light there might have been was rapidly fading. He was awake, he thought.

How many days ago was it, he wondered, when he'd last awakened feeling just like this? Still sleepy, feeling weak. After his accident. But *different* this time, too.

He wasn't hungry, at least not more than on a normal morning—or rather evening, the sun having just set completely—but then why should he be? Hadn't he eaten the weight of his whole body, or at least dreamed he had, then grown it back again—most of it anyway? He had read once that, in any process, there always was *some* waste.

So there would be less of him than when this had started. So much for behemoths.

But still—*some* monster. At least in his dream. It was wholly dark in his curtained bedroom, but he still felt—different. The weight, the heft, a sort of top-heaviness, strength here, weakness there, as he climbed out of bed. He seemed, at least, to still balance on two legs.

He tested the use of familiar and yet unfamiliar muscles, similar, too, in a generic sense, to what he had been used to. To what he *thought* he knew.

He lurched from the room, getting better, he thought, with each new step he made. Getting used to his balance. To swings, to counter-swings, thrusts and counterthrusts. To every action an equal reaction —he learned as if a child walking the first time. He knew how to walk, that is, yet it was *different.*

He shambled down the hall, immersed in pitch darkness, but learning grace with each step. Pulling memories now from some source other than what he thought he had once known. Memories he still had, though, guiding him to his apartment's bathroom, fingers, or some kind of pseudopods anyhow, reaching up to what might be his new mouth.

Feeling himself out.

He reached the bathroom. He felt for the sink, gripping its sides to turn to where he knew the bathroom mirror was. Gingerly, nervously, he reached his left hand out. He stretched to the light switch.

His middle finger.

He fumbled the switch on, and stared in the mirror at the face of Merryl.

✠

James Dorr *has two mostly short fiction collections* Strange Mistresses: Tales of Wonder and Romance *and* Darker Loves: Tales of Mystery and Regret *available from Dark Regions Press, while his all-poetry* Vamps (A Retrospective) *is just out in 2011 from Sam's Dot Publishing. An active member of SFWA and HWA with several hundred publications from* Alfred Hitchcock's Mystery Magazine *to* Xenophilia, *Dorr invites readers to visit his site at http://jamesdorrwriter.wordpress.com for current information and news.*

De'Atherton House

Sorrel Wood

I am not a writer. I am not at all a remarkable or interesting person and I am certainly not clever. Under normal circumstances the thought of precisely straightening a sheet of paper, pressing down upon the worn keys and hammering out a story would be abhorrent to me. However, I feel obliged, no compelled, to tell the truth about what happened the day I travelled to De'Atherton House, even though writing that name makes my fingers tremble. I am not a writer, but anybody who knows me would assure you that I am a truthful man and you must believe what I am about to describe. You must.

It was late autumn when the silent taxi driver dropped me at the front of that place. The trees were bare, their leaves strewn like rotting corpses across the lonely path, but the chilly sun seemed to mock the idea of trailing any light into the shady drive. The tall, iron gates were rusty and contorted into grotesque leers and it seemed as if they had not been opened for a long time. The road was silent and smelled musty and forgotten, but as I pressed against the gate and a screeching cry echoed throughout the estate I felt as though something was watching me.

I am not a superstitious man: indeed, I pride myself on my cerebral disposition and unshakeable rationality. But you must believe me when I confide that as I stepped through the gate of De'Atherton House, my senses were heightened to an animalistic intensity. The crunch of my feet against the rotting leaves was intolerably piercing to my ears and the slightest touch of my fingers against the rough iron was as chilling as death. The smell of moss and ivy was so mouldy that I could not breathe for retching and the sparkle of every cobweb glinted before my eyes. I have never attributed great weight to feelings, choosing instead to weigh up decisions according to their relative pros and cons. With every agonising step, though, a bestial instinct rose up inside me and gripped my heart like the sudden chill of a stormy wind: run. Turn around, run like a frightened animal, do not look back. Of course, I dismissed these thoughts as the childish whimsy of someone recovering from a long journey.

As I trod the overgrown pathway and noted how vicious creepers had angrily reclaimed crumbling stone ornaments, I tried to recall the last time I had actually seen Demelza De'Atherton. She was so quiet and strange that even though I had a vague recollection of her uncomfortable presence in the office, I struggled to pinpoint exactly when I had last felt the cold breeze as she walked past me. I am not known for being a sociable person in my office: I arrive at work precisely on time, work diligently at whichever documents need to be copied, edited or sorted and then leave at some hour in the evening. However, I always greet my colleagues in the office with a polite tip of my hat. When, occasionally, I glance and see a pale, thin-faced double of myself also furiously copying beneath a pile of yellowing papers, without exception I bestow upon them a generous smile and often make some comment about the weather or the daily commute. I understand that I am considered to be a dull, perhaps standoffish, but well-meaning and efficient member of the agency. I have worked there for many years.

Demelza De'Atherton was a different case altogether. She arrived to work early and was always the last to leave, to the extent that people whispered and joked that she slept amongst the papers. She certainly had the wild appearance of one who does not live a normal, measured existence: her hair was an explosion of wires at different lengths, as if she had been electrocuted and her skin was as deathly pale as if she never saw the light of the sun. Her eyes were crazed like an animal about to be attacked, or perhaps attack. They were big and beady, as though she was mad through lack of sleep. Demelza never spoke to anybody in the office, except for the occasional grunt and people soon gave up attempting to speak with her at all, collectively deciding that she was rude. Demelza had an erratic excuse to work: sometimes she would stare at the notice board in front of her as though she was in a trance. On other occasions she would attack her tasks with ferocity like a lion ripping apart its prey. Sometimes she would tear at papers with her nails, spill ink across them or screw them up with an erupting volcano of frustration. Often it would be me who was asked to stay late and rewrite her work, as it was useless to anybody, and the hours of copying her crazy handwriting sometimes made me feel a little unhinged and I would let out an angry cry, or a long, musical laugh. I am not a person easily troubled, but Miss De'Atherton made me feel uneasy.

When she was not tearing up papers, Demelza spoke loudly on the telephone to somebody named James. That is how I know all that I do about her (I am not nosey, but it was impossible not to hear her half of the conversation). She would shout and scream at James, slamming down the telephone and knocking over pots of pens. She once even threw her office chair across the room and knocked over her table, making a flurry of papers catch flight like butterflies. Some people thought James was her husband, others claimed he was her brother. I personally thought he might be a cousin. Whoever he was, I hope the poor man had strong nerves.

There were several mysteries surrounding Demelza. The first was why she was working at the office at all. It was well known that the De'Athertons were an old aristocratic family and that it was possible to walk from Oxford to Cambridge purely on De'Atherton land. There estate, it was rumoured, was so large that one could find themselves lost in the grounds forever. Their house, or rather castle (I am led to believe it was something between the two) had almost one thousand rooms and two people could live there and never see each other. Certainly, one could scream at the top of his lungs and never be heard. The first mystery, therefore, was why such a rich lady should need to find employment in an office in the first place. The second mystery was, given her conduct and inability to copy even a singular document without tearing it to pieces, how she managed to keep her job. The third mystery, in which I find myself inexplicably tied up, is why Demelza De'Atherton disappeared.

"Excuse me, Sir," I piped up one day in the office. The workers, with their translucent skin and long, bony noses, all stopped copying documents and turned their sneering eyes in my direction. There was an eerie silence. Nobody ever speaks to The Boss.

"Yes, Jenkins?" The back of The Boss's black hat said (he did not turn round).

"Actually, Sir," I quivered, "Actually Sir, it's Watkins."

"Yes, Jenkins?" He repeated more loudly, this time with a tightness to his tone.

I cleared my throat. "It's about Miss Demelza De'Atherton, Sir." The Boss turned around in his spinning office chair. His face was round, fat and pink and he had a moustache. He had big, bushy eyebrows and one of them was raised. "She's disappeared."

The Boss stood up. His black jacket and matching black trousers gave him the appearance of a large crow. "Has anyone seen Miss

Demelza De'Atherton?" He boomed. Everybody turned like mice back to their desks and scurried back to their writing. "When was the last time anybody saw her?" The scratching of busy pens and clicking of creaky typewriters became louder and faster. "Well, Jenkins," he said without looking at me. "I suppose you'd better go and see what's become of her."

"Me?" I squeaked, "Why me?" There was a general gasp, like a sudden gust of wind circulating the office. The Boss raised his eyebrow further, so it almost touched his forehead. "It's just that I don't know her!" I protested, "I don't even know where she lives."

"Don't be ridiculous Jenkins; everybody knows that Miss Demelza De'Atherton lives at De'Atherton House, somewhere between Oxford and Cambridge. Now call a taxicab and go there at once. And if you even think about charging the taxi to the company, it will be the last thing you do."

"But Sir, what about—"

"Your copying can wait."

As I walked the seemingly endless drive to the crumbling house, I mulled the events of the day over in my mind and felt slightly annoyed. However, the decrepit, demonic gargoyles glared at me with every step and the feeling was soon devoured by one of a vague, unidentifiable fear. I am sure, I mused, that there is a perfectly rational explanation for the woman's disappearance. She probably just decided to quit her job at the company. God knows the thought has occurred more than once in my mind and I am a long serving and reliable employee.

By the time I had reached the house it was completely dark save for a bright white moon sat high in the cloudless sky. It gave the house a spectral glow, as though it were not of this world. A trick of the senses, perhaps caused by the wind, meant that the faraway sound of howling in the forest (dogs, or perhaps foxes) seemed to be very close. I pulled my suit jacket tighter around my body. My skin felt prickly, but I think that it was merely a response to the cold, wet night.

The old, wooden door of the house towered above me and the bulky iron hinges swam before my eyes like insects. I hesitated, then pulled the frayed, damp cord off the heavy metal bell. Its clang was discordant as if angry at being disturbed. I stood on the stone doorstep for several minutes and shivered. The house certainly seemed unoccupied and it occurred to me that perhaps the family had abandoned it. Dilapidated manor houses were an expense and lacked modern conveniences; it was common these days for ancient families to relocate to more modern residences in town. I wondered whether Demelza would be annoyed to see me and think it rude, or whether she would even remember who I was.

Eventually the door opened with a disgruntled howl. I stepped forward into the thick shadow and at first I thought that nobody was there.

"Ye-es?" A thin and high-pitched voice whispered from the shadows. I presume it was a servant, although I never saw her face.

At first my voice croaked and stumbled in my throat because my mouth had become inexplicably dry. But then I removed my hat and said, "I'm here to see Miss De'Atherton. Please tell her it is Jeffrey Watkins from the office." The woman did not reply, but I discerned the movements of a hunched figure and heard the pat of footsteps, like the steps of an animal, slipping further away.

I have mentioned that I am not a curious person by nature, but I am observant and tend to remember what I have seen. As I stood alone in the dim hallway it occurred to me that I was most fortunate to be a guest at a place of such historical interest. The wide, sweeping hallway was grand but empty. There was a cavernous stone fireplace, buried in a thick layer of cobwebs and dust and a heavy suit of armour which was positioned at the exact angle to give the impression that it was staring at me. A wide, twisting staircase swept upwards towards the first floor. It was not to my taste: each dark wooden banister was gnarled and had been carved into the shape of an angry demon and the shadow pattern of the bars fell across the stairway giving the impression of a prison cell. Lining the wall there was a series of portraits, all painstakingly realistic and realised in dark oil paints. Each was of a woman in the De'Atherton ancestral line and they were copies of the pointed nose and beady eyed features of Demelza, or rather she was a copy of them. They all looked angrily watchful and their position behind the main window of the hallway meant that years of light had made them both fade into ghosts and also sharpened their peering glance.

Just as I was pondering these artifacts and making a copy of them in my mind, the figure of a bright white woman appeared at the top of the stairs. A flash of terror pierced through me, but then of course I realised that it was Demelza and that standing in front of the moonlight had made her appear to glow with ethereal translucence creating the illusion of a ghost.

"Miss De'Atherton," I said, bowing obsequiously. The grandeur of the surroundings impressed upon me the need to behave with the utmost courtesy. She glided towards me and smiled.

"Hello, Hawkins." Her manner was pleasant and relaxed and if she was surprised to see me, she did not show it. Time away from the office had clearly had a positive effect on the woman: her skin seemed brighter, her hair flatter and her pupils had ceased to bulge. Standing in the hallway of her ancestral house, she seemed like a perfectly normal, if aristocratic, woman. I felt a burning surge of guilt for the fantastical rumours that had circulated about her in the office.

I felt embarrassed and awkward for stumbling into the privacy of Miss De'Atherton's home. Certainly, I would hate it if someone from the office followed me home and discovered my secrets. "I've come from the office," I explained, looking at my polished black shoes. "You . . . you disappeared, Miss De'Atherton and we were concerned as to your whereabouts.

Her smile did not fade exactly, but it set in place like dried glue. "Yes," she said through her teeth. "Yes, well you see Mr. Hawkins, it became necessary to leave the office and return to De'Atheron House because James, my brother, was extremely ill. In fact," she took a sharp intake of breath through her teeth, "In fact I'm sorry to say that my brother has died." Her face froze into the same glazed stare as the ancestral portraits in the hallway.

"I'm very sorry to hear that, Miss De'Atherton," I said mechanically. I am not an emotional person and this kind of situation always makes me feel panicked. My cheeks flushed pink and it occurred to me that perhaps I should reach out and touch her arm, but there was something repellent about the throbbing veins in her transparent skin. Perhaps it would have been the wrong gesture entirely.

She stood in the pale moonlight like the statues in the garden. I waited for her to offer me a drink, or at least to invite me in to a drawing room, but I suppose with the grief and the fact that she had been alone for a while, not to mention her frosty manner at the best of times she did something that under normal circumstances would have seemed a bit peculiar. "Would you like to see him?"

I shuddered but then quickly recollected my sensibilities. I had already been unspeakably rude, arriving unannounced at the home of a grieving stranger. Demelza looked stonily composed, but I felt sorry for her. I decided that I had no option. "Certainly," I mumbled.

Demelza took a solitary candle and turned towards a dark doorway. We tiptoed down a gloomy stone staircase which twisted down into a cellar a long way below the ground. There was a series of stone arches and the cold, lightless passageway became increasingly narrow. I knew that it was fairly common for ancient families to have crypts in which generations of ancestors lay silently and resisted decay. I had not given much thought to what such places felt like.

The cold stone walls seemed to press down and against us. Rows of horizontal figures lay beneath cold shrouds like cakes beneath napkins or children sleeping in bunk beds. I imagined them all with the same pointed nose and beady features of the De'Atherton family; a hundred frozen Demelzas lined up in a row like toy soldiers. If I were not such a rational man I might have entertained the notion that one of the figures turned its head beneath the sheet.

Demelza paced coolly to the end of the row and lifted the paper-thin wisp of cloth that had been resting over James De'Atherton. "Say hello to James," she said.

Mr. James De'Atherton was a carbon copy of his deathly pale sister. He had the same angular features, like a pecking bird. I had expected his eyes to be closed as though in a peaceful sleep, but they were open and glassy like marbles.

"Good evening, Mr. De'Atherton," I said nervously. I am not sure why; it was whimsical and out of character.

Demelza stood in the silence, letting the candle burn down to the wick. It flickered wildly, making a dazzling light show of spectres on the wall. I felt like suitable time had elapsed and that we should turn back towards the land of the living. However, Demelza was resolutely fixed to the hard stone floor. She showed no sign of movement.

I am a sensible person and pride myself on my sound judgment; I beg you to believe what I am about to relate. Without prior warning there was a low, harrowing moan and a shuffling sound. I spun around to face the corpse of Mr. James De'Atherton. Demelza's eyes flickered but she did not flinch.

All of a sudden, James De'Atherton turned his head, fixed his bulging eyes in our direction and raised his pale arm. I screamed.

"Miss De'Atherton," I stammered, "Miss De'Atherton- your brother is not dead!"

"Oh," she said, "he's quite dead. You must be having a funny turn, Jenkins. People of a certain sensitive nature find places such as this one offensive to their sensibilities.

Mr. James De'Atherton lurched towards us with his withered arm.

"Miss De'Atherton," I said breathlessly, "Miss De'Atherton I really must leave!"

Demelza turned towards me like a dressmaker's dummy on wheels. "Mr. Hopkins, you are not going anywhere."

"But," My eyes bulged and I bit my lip. "The taxi is waiting and I really must go."

She sneered and let out a sinister snort from the side of her mouth that reminded me of when I used to work with her in the office. "The taxi has gone," she announced with the faintest trace of a laugh.

The corpse, or ghost, or perhaps live figure of Mr. James De'Atherton leant towards me with a bestial cry of horror. Making a snap decision, which is unusual for my character, I pushed Miss De'Atherton, sending her flying with such force that she flew across the crypt and cracked her head on its ancient stone wall. Then, with no doubt in my mind that she was lying dead on the floor amongst generations of her family, I left my hat and jacket and ran. I ran like a fox pursued by bloodhounds, leaving that foul, crazed woman to bleed to death on the floor. You must believe me when I tell you that I had no other choice.

✠

Sorrel Wood is an English and Drama teacher in Cambridge, England. Before training as a teacher she studied English Literature at Durham University. Sorrel has had several poems and short stories published in Internet journals and enjoys sharing creative writing with the students at her school.

Visions

Neil Kloster

No man or woman alive could claim that Frederic Le'Charmine's work was not only exquisite, but that his paintings were positively lifelike. The talented artisan came to the city of Paris during the summer months in search of something that he described only as, "picturesque visions of the flesh," women so beautiful that they were the only ones that he desired to paint. So much so, that at his latest unveiling, he professed aloud that he had plucked out his eyes from their sockets with the sharp wooden end of his painters brush. Naturally, upon hearing such a claim, especially from one who had painted such visually stunning works of art, a person would consider that their hearing had failed them immensely. But alas, the statement proved true, as Le'Charmine revealed to a small crowd of curious onlookers that underneath his jaded green spectacles—with side glasses to protect his sunken hulls from the influence of light—that his eyes no longer occupied their usual vacancy within his skull.

Gasps of horrified shock rose from their lips as they stared at the man, who only moments ago stood in front his masterful depiction of a lovely young woman, and commented so brilliantly about the detail to her golden locks as if his sight still were marvelously intact.

When asked about his extremely brash and gruesome act of self-mutilation, the painter explained himself calmly to the crowd that, "I needn't *eyes* to see *true* beauty, but only my fingers to stroke the brush. These optics - you all fear are indispensable - yet through my work, do I not convince you that my vision is even more penetrating than your own?"

Rows of applause echoed in the air as fans, onlookers and critics alike all applauded and cheered for Le'Charmine: the stranger with no eyes, yet whose hand and brush saw more than even a thousand eyes could even begin to attempt.

The air of his story lay thick with mystery and intrigue, there was no doubt, and yet there was no comparison, Le'Charmine's work greatly surpassed any artist whose work even dared attempt to gain stage in the galleries that season, or gain any recognition or status at all during those warm summer months. He was, in fact, the *only* artist that lived on the lips of critics and art lovers alike.

Like wildfire, rumors broke and ran wild about the mysterious painter: Who was he? Where did he come from? What school of study did he subscribe to and perhaps the most entertained inquiry of them all, how did he continue to capture his subjects' loveliness so vividly *without sight*?

One night, as Le'Charmine sat reclusively, engorging himself on wine at the Weingut Cobenzl, he quickly became one of many entertained by the harmonic vocals of the tavern owner's lovely young daughter, Eliza. Her youthful voice radiated a sound so lovely that it ensnared the often barbarous and ruthless drunkards of the night, and lulled them into a soft purring trance of calm esthetic peace. Large brutish men sat like playful kittens, pining over the angelic barmaid that swooned past them singing her delightful tune.

That night, Le'Charmine needn't see the face of the woman, whose voice lured him in not unlike the mythical sirens of old, to know that she was truly one worthy of his brush and that he must hastily, make her acquaintance.

He rose from his table and — be it true that he could not see — found her amongst his own personal darkness and met her charming voice with his own. The two lingering melodies met and found each other like beacons among the darkness, bringing each of them closer together, interwoven beautifully.

Patrons that night of the Weingut Cobenzl sat astonished. Not only did this mysterious stranger possess the astonishing ability to give his paintings life without sight, a miracle reserved by none other than God himself. But by *Jove*, his voice resonated throughout the air with notes written by angels, delivered through his lips and sung into life like none other before him.

The scene was euphoric.

She found herself tethered to him, his song; the very leash that linked them both together.

Upon the culmination of their serenade, Le'Charmine and the beautiful Eliza took their bows in front of a very appreciative, if not slightly inebriated jury of clamoring onlookers.

It was not until later that both Le'Charmine and the lovely Eliza disappeared from the main stage of the taverns nightly festivities. They sat together. Le'Charmine offered Eliza a goblet of wine and begged her to accompany him for the rest of the evening, "Mademoiselle, you must drink with me. For how would such an act be taken for you to deny your own father's vintage merlot in his *own tavern?*"

She took the goblet in between her delicate fingers and held it to her pursed rose-colored lips, pretending to sip, then placed the goblet back in front of Le'Charmine as she replied, "There. Now we will never know, will we?"

They both laughed.

Eliza leaned further. Le'Charmine could feel her weight resting on the opposite end of the table, "So tell me painter, how does one capture such elegant beauty, if you cannot even see the goblet that still sits filled, resting at your fingertips?"

Le'Charmine grinned and replied, "What makes you believe that I know not that the goblet is still filled?" He snatched it up with such speed that Eliza almost forgot that the man had no eyes to see. He put it to his nose, sniffed then drank the rest of Eliza's merlot down in one smooth sip.

Eliza basked wildly in awe and applauded while Le'Charmine shouted for another bottle.

"Bartender!" he cried, "*Barolo;* your very best bottle for myself and my enchanting guest!"

The bartender sauntered over, carrying a bottle of Barolo cradled in his arm, wrapped in a dark vermillion cloth.

"Father!" Eliza cried, "You must meet Monsieur Frederic Le'Charmine. He is the man who created those breathtaking works of art. Monsieur Frederic, allow me to introduce you to Andre Martan, my father and owner of the Weingut Cobenzl."

"Ah, the painter!" Andre said, "Welcome to my tavern monsieur. A true pleasure."

Le'Charmine rose from his seat, bowed and said, "Monsieur, please the pleasure is all mine; allow me to formally introduce myself. As your lovely daughter has already unveiled, my name is Frederic Le'Charmine, but in regards to my profession, she is too kind. I am only a mere painter. One who is only *inspired* by beauty," he then looked over to Eliza and nodded, "but does not *create* it."

"So humble, isn't he papa?" Eliza said.

"Quite so, *quite* so. Monsieur, I have seen your talent first hand and be it that I am no critic, yet I confess that none other could paint such breathtaking visions the way that you have managed to capture."

"You flatter me monsieur."

Andre then took the bottle of Barolo out from the cradle of his arm and handed it to Le'Charmine.

"Come; let us drink to your celebrity! I understand that rumors of your paintings are reaching far across France. You would do me the honor of accepting this bottle as a token of my friendship as we toast to your success, no?"

Le'Charmine smiled, but held up his hand.

"Monsieur Martan, your flattery and your hospitality know no bounds, yet I must refuse your all too gracious offer."

Andre's face grew long and Eliza's eyes widened with maddening surprise.

"Monsieur?" Andre inquired.

"I can only accept your gracious gift and your generosity *only* on the agreement that you allow me the opportunity to capture your daughter's radiance on the cloth of my canvas."

Eliza sighed and put a hand to her chest, "Monsieur, I-I would be honored!"

"As would *I!*" Andre proclaimed proudly and then finally handed Le'Charmine the bottle of Barolo. "Come; let us drink upon this merry occasion!"

They uncorked the bottle of Barolo and poured the dark vermillion wine into three glass goblets and clinked them together as Andre toasted, "Here's to you Frederic Le'Charmine. To your marvelous works to date," and then looked over to Eliza, "and to your even more marvelous works to come!"

Eliza blushed as Andre and Le'Charmine tapped their goblets against her own with a resonating clink and proceeded to sip.

"Tomorrow," Le'Charmine said, "I will come back and if I am able to even capture only a small amount of your ravishing daughters beauty on canvas, then I will finally consider my existence as a painter a success."

The artisan kept firm to his word as he returned later the next night to the Weingut Cobenzl after hours. The tavern sat calm and undisturbed, a serene juxtaposition from the lively scenes the night before.

Upstairs, Eliza sat patiently as Le'Charmine set up his easel and brushes.

"Monsieur…" Eliza said.

"Yes?"

"Might I inquire upon something that has still perplexed me since we met?"

Le'Charmine smirked as he continued to set up.

"You want to know how I will paint you ...when I cannot *see* you, is that it?"

Eliza replied, "Why, yes."

He then uncovered several tiny jars of varying degree of size and color. He unfastened the lid to one that held a blue colored substance inside, walked over to Eliza, and held it to her nose.

"It smells like berries, fresh wild blueberries. What is it?"

He then held the jar to his own nose and took in a deep breath of the same scent.

"Paint. Made of my own design. It is a very special blend of herbs, fruits and other ingredients; this is what helps me capture one's beauty so vividly onto my canvas. I can smell the sweet scent of the blueberry in my blue oceans, the musk of the pine in my emerald green and the lingering sting of cinnamon in my auburn shade."

"But how can you paint something that you cannot see?"

"My dear, doth the worm need eyes to see?" He professed. "No, it relies on what it knows, what it senses and, more importantly, what it can *feel* to in order to slither itself around deep into the cold wet depths of the earth."

With his free hand, he brushed the soft flesh of her cheek with his forefinger then walked over to his easel. His touch was cold and sent an icy shiver through her, prickling her skin with gooseflesh.

He dipped his brush into one of the large glass jars and began to paint.

Eliza sat patiently, as still and as calm as a sculpture as she watched Le'Charmine stroke his brush back and forth against the canvas. With no eyes to guide it, his hand appeared possessed, commanded by some unseen force and yet, perfectly capable in the least of maneuvering the canvas. He worked diligently over the piece, meticulously pining over every minute detail, giving every brunette strand of hair that sat on Eliza's head his most due attention.

However, with every stroke, Eliza felt her strength beginning to ebb from her body. She began to feel weak, discombobulated; regardless of how proper and statuesque she presented herself.

The moment where Le'Charmine was finally able to unveil his latest masterpiece, Eliza nearly fell from her wooden stool with gasping exhaustion. She trembled; her flesh had softened to the pale color of white parchment, as if her very life had seeped out of her.

"Eliza!" Andre cried as he rushed over to catch his frail daughter, "My child, what is wrong?"

"It...It's nothing," she muttered, smiling at her caring father, "I'm fine papa, I'm fine. Please monsieur, is it finished? May I see it?"

Le'Charmine put down his brush, the bristles caked in thick brown paint.

"It is."

Eliza, with the aid of her father, slowly crept towards the front side of the canvas.

Upon that moment, Eliza's eyes brightened as Andre gasped in amazement and in awe of Le'Charmine's fantastic reflection of his beautiful daughter.

"Monsieur!" Eliza cried, "It's...It's amazing! Why, I dare confess to you that your vision looks even better than myself!"

"You are far too kind," Le'Charmine replied, "but in order to capture beauty, *true* beauty; one must be so lucky as to have such a lovely specimen such as yourself to mimic. Without *your* loveliness mademoiselle, my work is not possible."

Eliza's cheeks blushed with rose-colored flavor in response to Le'Charmine's compliment.

"It is absolutely breathtaking monsieur, absolutely breathtaking," Andre professed.

Le'Charmine bowed his head, "Thank you monsieur, you are too kind." Then turned his head towards Eliza, "And now, I must leave you. You are not well, as you said, and therefore, you must rest. I thank you for this pleasure, to paint such a ravishing and lovely creature. You have both been so kind and inviting, but now I must continue my travels throughout Europe; but Paris, she has been so kind to me, that I feel I cannot resist her charms. I will return back through your land and hope to call upon you both again, but now my dear, if I may be so bold, I fear that you need to rest."

"The gentleman is correct," Andre said. "Excuse us monsieur whilst I see my daughter to her room."

"Of course."

"My apologies monsieur," Eliza said softly, "I am truly embarrassed. I do not know what has overtaken me so suddenly."

"Mademoiselle, cast away any notion or thought of fear that you may have tainted the vision that I have of you. There is no need for your apology, nor your embarrassment; banish the thought away quickly. Now, take your loving father's hand and let him walk you to your quarters. Remember mademoiselle: it is only through your beauty that I can truly live.

I thank you again for your gracious gift and only hope to see you again, perhaps even more ravishing than ever ...if such a thing be possible?

She smiled, "Good night painter."

"Good night," he replied.

After attending to Eliza, Andre thanked the painter for his kind words and company and then wished him farewell on his journey. Le'Charmine thanked the gracious tavern owner once again for the gift of his daughter's exquisite radiance. He then turned and walked into the midnight air and swiftly disappeared from Andre and Eliza's existence.

Days followed and Eliza's dreadful condition progressively continued to worsen. She lay in bed, pale as cotton and as still as a statue. Her eyes, no longer those of the loving and vibrant creature that Le'Charmine had captured only a few short nights ago, but now they appeared distant, hazy — as if one were to look through a thin layer of icy white mist. Her pale flesh burned red with fever while beads of heavy sweat collected themselves upon her brow like morning dew.

With every passing hour, Eliza's strength ebbed and her breathing grew shallow until, on the third night of her sickness, her body, which lay severely emaciated and already ravaged by her illness, drew its last breath and ceased its function not quite past the eleventh hour.

Due to the fear of contamination from whatever strange sickness possessed it, Eliza's once youthful body, still wrapped in her own bed sheets, now lay reduced to nothing more than a pile of crackling black ashes and charred bones that sat steaming underneath a smoldering pyre.

Amidst the vast congregation of spectators that had gathered within the Galerie le' Gevaudon, the unveiling of Marseille's newest and most sought after talent: Monsieur Frederic Le'Charmine was a spectacle of epic dimension. People from all around, who have heard of the mysterious and mystical painter, who created stunning works of art without the services of his eyes, flocked to the gallery in hopes of catching even the smallest glimpse of his presence.

The show proved a success as offers for the painters work flowed freely like wine.

Upon the cessation of the nights' festivities, the locked gallery floor sat dark and baron like a crypt as its thick marble walls entombed the acclaimed painter's portraits with unwavering security.

However, soft voices echoed from beyond the walls. The halls within the Galerie le' Gevaudon now held a cacophony of faint ghostlike whispers, each spectral voice resonate of a woman once painted by Le'Charmine himself, but now long since dead.

Among the works, hung a portrait of startling beauty, a newer piece; truly one of the shows more illustrious and admired works of

Le'Charmine's genius: the portrait of a young woman, with soft velvety brown hair and dark rose-colored lips.

Within its canvas, a haunting voice rang aloud.

"*Papa?*"

"Where are you? Please, help me. I don't know where I am. It's dark and I'm *so* very cold."

"Papa…?"

"*PAPA!*"

Neil Kloster *has published several stories in magazines such as* House of Horror, Sex and Murder *and* Death Rattle Magazine. *Neil currently works, paints and lives in Aurora, IL with his girlfriend Alissa, a human skull that sits on his desk and never helps him (unless he begs for it) and his vast collection of Spiderman memorabilia. Visit him at www.neilkloster.wordpress.com or follow him on Twitter @NeilKolster*

The Final Sculpture

Ian Shoebridge

In south-eastern France, where the land starts to become violently hilly — as though preparing itself for its sudden upward surge into the great Alps — it is still possible to find forgotten villages and hilltop châteaux, and forget for a while the burden of one's own history and times.

I came to Europe in search of inspiration. A certain species of gloom had infiltrated my imagination and robbed me of the alchemical ability for artistic creation. This melancholia had so far resisted other cures. I hoped the bracing change of scenery might revive my enthusiasm.

I found myself visiting a lesser-known château overlooking a small town near the Alps. Briefly adapted as a royal retreat, the interior was alternately bare and lavish, with every kind of decorative exorbitance when it had any.

I had followed some steps down into the royal crypt. The coffins here were detailed with all manner of fantastic images: skulls, wraiths, weeping maidens, long curved swords with decorated hilts, wreaths of black iron flowers, death masks.

It was as I marveled at these morbid flights of imagination and pondered on the paradox of the loving care with which they seemed to have been prepared, that the strange Frenchman spoke to me, giving an odd smile.

"I notice you seem deeply engrossed by these carvings," he told me. "They are, yes, quite beautiful — if you have a taste for it."

I told him, "I'm wondering why modern artworks often seem to lack this awe-inspiring quality."

He nodded. "Brutality, of course," he announced abruptly. "Many of history's greatest artworks were made by slaves, or people who were under the threat of death—which amounts to slavery. They were rigidly trained in their art and socially accepted motifs; they had no room for real, individual self-expression. These coffins before us are no exception."

Shaking my head with vehemence, I felt obliged to argue: "It is when the artist feels a genuine devotion to the cause that the work is imbued with some intangible, timeless element we understand as sincerity..."

He laughed. "This is not a separate thing from slavery and oppression; it is separate only from individual expression. You can't argue that something created under deplorable conditions excludes its qualification as good art, or else you are excluding most of what human endeavour has created. The ideology you adhere to is entirely new: it evolved only after kingdoms had crumbled, religions had declined and class systems lost relevance."

"Well, think of religious art..." I began.

"Religious art!" exclaimed the Frenchman with a derisive laugh. "Don't you see that once again, this is not the product of devotion so much as of brutality? The church was the greatest instrument of oppression history has seen. It was manipulated by wealthy archbishops into an opiate of ignorance for the populace, with fear of hell to chastise on the inside, and holy wars and burning of heretics to purge on the outside. There is no real individuality in these religious works—a thousand images of a crucified savior—they might as well be produced on a factory line."

"Then this is what troubles me," I said. "How can brutality, cruelty and oppression produce something beautiful—something more lasting than what we've created in times of freedom?"

The enigmatic Frenchman smiled. "These are interesting thoughts that consume you," he said, and gave a laugh that made me uncomfortable. "Perhaps you would be interested in seeing my private collection? I live in the Château Douleur, not far from here."

✠

The weary intensity of his manner had intrigued me, and in the afternoon I caught a bus into the hills. By the time I reached the short, stately mansion a long, grey cloud had cast a dreary shadow over the fading afternoon. The tall stranger was expecting me and showed me into the lavish interiors. I remarked that a clear day must afford spectacular views of the French Alps.

"Yes, you can see the Swiss Alps from here," he said. "We are very near the border here, near the old road tunnel in fact."

"I don't remember seeing a tunnel on the map," I said.

"It is closed now. There was a dreadful accident, about eleven years back. Many people were killed. It was horrible. They were unable even to clear the wreckage from the tunnel. It has remained closed ever since. There was talk of building a new one, but nothing has come of it."

My host was silent, and throughout the tour of the château retained his air of melancholy resignation, like one harbouring a heavy secret or fatally morbid outlook on existence, but now and then would beam in obscure delight at some amusement.

The château, having remained in private ownership, was remarkably well preserved, with some of the most extravagant furnishings I had seen so far. Grim paintings, ostensibly originals, such as *Death and the Maiden*, myriad morbid *vanitas*, works by Johannes Torrentius and austere etchings by Piranesi decorated the walls. Vaulted ceilings created a tessellating effect that was dizzying, like glancing down corridors of infinity, adding to the overall imposing architecture.

Finally, he led me down a long spiral staircase, so steep in its descent that one had to constantly turn to avoid slipping, and so narrow as to admit only one person for some distance. Then through a great wooden door we entered the horrific gallery.

It was several minutes before I could even speak. The appalling tower rose in the center of the room like a tortured plant, up to the skylight where a few stray drops of rain were collecting from the brooding afternoon storm. Around the unspeakable creation was the protective rail. Along the wall were presented historical documents. There was nothing else in the ghastly chamber.

"Well...what are your thoughts?" asked my host quietly.

"I think it's dreadful." I said. "What do you expect me to say?" I gave another sickened look at the monstrous creation in the center, hardly able to believe my eyes. "Is this what you meant about artworks being the product of brute force?"

"Originally, yes: slaves were bought, and forcibly committed to this grim work of art. After slavery became unacceptable, the benefactors of this obscure historical project continued its development in secret. Selected persons from particular families were brainwashed into willingly becoming part of it—when their time came. Imagine how thorough a devotion is required for that! This is what I meant. These people, their sacrifice, can't be disregarded for the…snobbish criticism that they had no choice in it."

"But this doesn't still go on, does it?" I asked with concern.

"Not in the same way. Still, this disturbing tradition left a legacy of martyrdom — a cult of religious masochism — that brought many more people, even to this day, willingly sacrificing their lives for the privilege of becoming part of this. Now we have governments and churches electing volunteers from the many applications we receive."

"I can't believe it," I said. "It's disgusting."

"You look sickened, but consider what a feat it would be to give your life to this thing voluntarily. Imagine the pain, the pull on your limbs, the devotion to the cause you would need to be able to do this. This is simply not something you could commit to without the most fanatic and sincere intent. And for that, this creation cannot be so quickly disregarded."

I was trying not to imagine it. The agonized expressions still evident on the skulls — hopeless devotion and eternal anguish; the delicate postures of the victims; the careful structuring so that in some places the different bones literally flowed in and out of each other like interweaving vines. The thousand dreams that never took flight because their owners were bound up so. There was nothing that could be said about such a creation.

The Frenchman regarded it with melancholy philosophy. "It is grim, it is morbid, yes; but in its savage way it is beautiful too. For what else does it express but our own frailty and mortality; the very agonies of life itself; the struggle of every living organism to grow and exist in a wild, savage world? By your own tastes this is a good artwork. It says far more than the dry aesthetics of a palace; the unoriginal Chinese-whispers of a thousand crucifixion images; a history of forgotten martyrs. This is the true history of the world, right here, and it is sick and twisted only as much as it is beautiful and hopeful, and sad, and above all: real."

"Why did you bring me here?" I asked.

He shrugged. "I wanted you to see it. I thought you may understand it. And…I do not know. For I am the last in my family line, and maybe the next person the government elects to caretake will not show the same respect. He will open it up to the general public and sell tickets, so fat tourists can photograph their friends climbing over the decades of bones; sell out the remaining spaces to rich international businessmen and brutal foreign dictators seeking immortality through art."

I said fearfully, "And my part in this? Are you expecting me to commit my involvement?"

"Don't be so melodramatic. You came of your own free will. So too you may leave, if you can truly declare that it doesn't intrigue you."

"Then I choose to leave," I said. "If this is the ultimate conclusion of all artistic expression: a towering heap of skeletons."

I left the château, without looking back. I waited impatiently on the edge of the road for the first bus I saw away from there. By now it was early evening, and thick grey clouds suggested more rain. At last, a rumbling old vehicle with no other passengers pulled up. We started, winding a way through dramatic hills. I looked out the windows for the familiar lights of the town, but we seemed to be heading more for the dark line of mountains. I started to worry, uncertain of the way back to the town at this late hour. I looked out the window for any specific landmark or signpost, but could see nothing. We were past the settled areas, right at the foot of the wild mountain range, and only scattered, lonely cottages evidenced civilization. We hadn't passed another car for some distance.

I assured myself I must merely have caught the wrong bus. But even as I rose to speak to the driver we turned a sharp corner and faced a broad wall of rock, which there was no way around, or over. The foothills of the immense mountain range itself loomed up above us, and then I saw that the road ahead disappeared into a dark tunnel right through the mountain. I ran up to the front of the bus.

"I thought this old tunnel was closed!" I said to the driver.

He puzzled over my words, then, remembering some English, said at last, "No, not closed, no. It was re-opened a few years ago. We go this way because the other road is much longer."

"I don't want to go this way," I said, panicking more than I could account for. "Please let me off here."

"Don't be silly, there is nothing around here. You would be stranded, in the middle of nowhere. It is even about to rain. Don't be silly."

"No, I have to get off!" I demanded, sweating in sudden fear. The bus driver shook his head and ignored me. I sat down helplessly in the seat behind him, beginning to shake with apprehension.

As we drew closer, I noticed something else, something far worse. Road barriers, warning signs, flashing past. The bus driver had lied. The tunnel wasn't open at all. The ghostly outline of wrecked, scorched vehicles began to materialize in the dim, up ahead. I watched the approaching tunnel mouth with rising fear.

Ian Shoebridge *writes mostly short fiction, some of which has appeared in* Bound For Evil, Electric Velocipede, Subtle Edens *and the upcoming* Where are We Now? *anthology. He is highly arachnophobic and prefers rainy weather. He lives in Sydney, Australia.*

Sufletul Mortii

Tom Sawyer

It was an artistic piece of sinister beauty. A portrait that was painted in the colors of blood, evil, malevolence, and death. Speaking of futures past and of times not yet conceived or dreamt of.

It was timeless.

Darkness emanated from it. Yet it seduced the eyes that beheld it.

It went by many descriptions. All of them the same in its many trails and journeys throughout the ages and its temporary destinations.

Even the portrait's name, *Sufletul Mortii*, Romanian for *Soul Eater*, echoed its dark nature.

And it bore witness to history.

To kings and tyrants—war, famine, death and destruction. It was present to it all, getting richer and more vivid in color with each tragedy.

It brought forth ruin and death to all who possessed it. The portrait could never be owned, only purchased for a time. In turn, it owned a piece of each person that beheld it.

No artist was ever known. Though many speculated it was painted by the Devil himself, with the blood and souls of man.

It yearned to be found and admired. It wasn't particular to who its admirers were. It could entrance almost anyone.

We came across it quite by accident. We sought shelter in a decrepit, old monastery from a tumultuous storm during our trip across Europe. They heavy rains had washed out the bridge to the town ahead; a large tree had become uprooted and blocked the road behind us.

While aged and dilapidated, there still remained a few wooden benches, chairs, and pews. We called out to announce our presence.

There was no answer.

As the storm raged outside we became acclimated to our new but temporary surroundings and began to explore the place.

Cautiously, we opened doors to other rooms, long since deserted and only host to memories and ghosts.

Constance and Veronica clung to us closely for protection and reassurance. While there were no signs of occupancy, we didn't feel alone. There was a darkness present other than the mid-day storm that interrupted our journey.

At last we explored a back room and cellar area. It was there in the back room that we found what would be the source of our worst nightmares.

We opened the door, and the first thing that caught our attention was the enormous life-size oval portrait on the wall.

Upon seeing it, Constance screamed.

Its image was so life-like and visceral.

It was perhaps the most disturbing piece of artwork I had ever been witness to.

What we beheld was a portrait that was filled with and radiated evil. No. It was evil, unlike any kind I had ever seen. We stood before it, studying it, as it hung there studying us in return. It felt like it was boring into our souls.

My friend, Peter, commented that it was sinister. Mesmerizing. Horrid yet enticing.

I don't remember how much time we spent entranced by it. The portrait seemed so horrifyingly real we could hardly move.

I finally found the strength to turn away.

It was then I noticed in a large chair, the skeletal remains of what had once been a priest. He, or rather his skeleton, lay in his ceremonial robes. Next to him on the floor was an old, thick leather bound book.

Constance and Peter turned around, and when she saw the robed corpse, she screamed. Her shock echoed in the empty monastery.

Yet her loud echoing scream had no affect on Veronica. It didn't even faze her as she kept staring at the portrait. I went over and picked up the book. As I opened it, and turned the pages I realized it was about the portrait.

We left, seeking the safer confines of the sanctuary. Peter had to grab Veronica and physically move her; she was so mesmerized by it.

Waiting for the storm to pass, I began to read aloud from the book. It was troublesome at times, trying to decipher the old and faded Edwardian script. But I finally managed:

> "The portrait was commissioned by Vlad Drakulya, later known as the infamous Vlad the Impaler. He desired a portrait to hang in the main hall of his castle. He demanded that the portrait be so terrifyingly real that it would instantly instill fear and horror amongst friend and foe alike."

I paused and looked at the others, uncertain until they nodded for me to continue:

> "The artist, unknown only to Vlad, sent with it an emissary as a present. Vlad accepted the portrait with joy and gratitude. The emissary told Vlad that the portrait had been painted with the blood of his enemies. That it was worked in not only oils, but death, fear, and all the nightmares that existed with man."

I continued to read:

> "Vlad cherished it. Ironically Vlad would fall prey to its horror and malevolence as well."

Then I noticed the writing style changed. I couldn't make out the lettering, but it I guessed it looked as if it were written in Latin. I tried to read it, but couldn't.

Some of the writing was too indistinguishable to read.

Finally I came across another legible passage:

> "The portrait, Sufletul Mortii, was given as a gift to Elizabeth Bathory, the Blood Countess of Hungary, on her twenty-first birthday."

"Who was Elizabeth Bathory?" Constance asked.

I continued to read:

> "The portrait was hung in the room where legend states she murdered some six hundred and fifty victims. The portrait continued to hang in the sealed wing where the Countess remained in exile until her death."

I started to notice a trend with this huge oval portrait, the *Sufletul Mortii*. The portrait was always around death, destruction, bloodshed, and evil.

"Keep reading," Peter said.

"The portrait surfaced again in Germany during the Thirty Years War between the Catholics and the Lutherans. It was captured and taken to Charles the fifth of the Holy Roman Empire where it was hidden away. He could not stand the portrait, rumors indicated he feared it, and sent it to France – away from the Vatican."

I then came across more of the text in a language I couldn't name nor read, thus I was forced to skip ahead delving further into the book:

"The portrait became a gift to Louis the sixteenth and was later handed down to Napoleon Bonaparte. Both men were in possession of the Sufletul Mortii unto their destruction and deaths."

An old blood stain smeared the handwriting over the next paragraph.

After a few moments I was finally able to decipher another section and started to read once again:

"It was in the possession of Archduke Franz Ferdinand of Austria. The Archduke's assassination was the catalyst that set off World War One."

I scanned the next paragraph, my eyes catching word of a name well known to history. I paused.

"What does the last paragraph say, Christopher?" Constance asked.

"When the Germans under the newly elected fuehrer reunified Austria as part of Germany, the German Army took over and annexed the country. Kurt Schuschnigg, a Nazi sympathizing Austrian Chancellor, gave the portrait – the Sufletul Mortii – to his friend and ally the Fuhrer, Adolph Hitler."

There was no writing after that. We could only conclude it had been here ever since.

When I stopped reading, we noticed Veronica was gone. While I was reading from the book, the three of us had become distracted.

We immediately knew where she had gone.

An uncomfortable silence filled the room as a chill went through us. Peter agreed to go and check on her, while Constance and I stayed in the sanctuary.

A few minutes later, we heard an ungodly scream, a mixture of sheer terror and gut wrenching pain.

Fighting back fear, we headed towards the source of the scream. Peter was on the floor, on his knees sobbing like an inconsolable child. It was then we noticed Veronica. It was no longer her. Her clothes merely covered what was left of her skeletal remains. Constance shrieked.

I glanced at the portrait. Something about it had changed. It was already life-like, but now it seemed almost alive. I moved closer to it, being cautious, but kept what I thought was a safe distance. For a moment, I thought I could hear soft cries—distant and faint—coming from it. But then I reasoned my imagination was getting the best of me. Standing closer, I could sense the terrible darkness coming from the portrait. It had changed.

Its power had grown.

I knew we had to leave as soon as possible. Though I couldn't understand it, I knew we were in danger if we stayed here. Especially in the portrait room. Turning away, I thought I had heard a deep guttural sound, a kind of death growl.

I sensed that the portrait was the embodiment of evil. Alive and awaiting its next victim.

I told Constance to help me grab Peter, and get out of the room. The both of us helped Peter out of there.

Uncertain of what Peter had seen, it couldn't have been good. His body trembled as we led him out.

Back in the sanctuary, we sat down, trying to make sense of it all. I knew that we had to leave, but the storm was just too bad.

After a few minutes, Peter had regained his self-control. He began to tell us what happened, that he knew she was somehow mesmerized by the painting.

When he entered the room, he saw her standing there. As he walked towards her, he noticed a large, dark, shadowy presence that reached out towards her. It pulled out a translucent image of her spirit out of her physical body, and pulled it into the painting.

He reached out to touch her body, and she shriveled before him, collapsing to the floor in a heap of clothed bones. It was then that we heard him scream.

I didn't doubt him, but I didn't know what to think either. I knew I didn't want to stay here, but the weather was dictating our present travel plans.

The raging storm caused the old monastery to shake and rattle. The lights inside were growing dimmer as the day had progressed and the storm grew worse. We looked around, managing to find a few old oil lamps. Even with the additional light, we weren't any more comfortable.

At least we were sheltered and dry.

Peter was adamant that the portrait was evil and needed to be destroyed. He was positive it was alive. He thought it fed off of misery and evil that existed with its former owners, like Vlad the Impaler, Elizabeth Bathory, and Adolph Hitler. It fed off them until they had outlived their usefulness.

It was like a cancerous abomination that just took over and changed those who had it. It was not witness to history but part of it, helping to influence it.

I told Peter I would help him destroy it. Once the storm passed, we could burn it with the oil lamps and leave this God-forsaken place. He agreed.

We sat and discussed what our options were. Peter was upset and pacing around. After a few minutes, Constance and I noticed he was missing.

Instinctively we both knew where he was. We had hoped he hadn't suffered the same fate as Victoria.

We found him outside the closed door to the room.

He raised his index finger to his lips indicating we needed to be quiet and pay attention. We both listened intently, but heard nothing.

"You didn't hear that," Peter asked.

All three of us stood quietly, listening for whatever it was he had heard, but we were only met with silence. Silence and the furious storm raging outside.

A look of defeated resignation spread across his face. While we believe he had heard something coming from the room, we feared whatever it had been was working hard to seriously unnerve him.

We tried in vain to get him to return with us, but he refused. He was obsessed with hearing whatever was coming from the room that held the portrait.

I feared for our lives and our sanity.

We wondered if this storm would ever subside enough to let us leave. In the course of just a few hours, we had lost one member of our group to some dark, diabolical force and another was gradually losing his mind.

I returned to the book, to see if there was any clue to what could help protect ourselves from its malicious evil. Meanwhile, Constance had gone off to check on the storm.

As I flipped through the pages, a separate piece of paper fell out. I quietly began to read:

> To whomever is reading this, my name is Brother Frederick. I am a member of the Order of the Sacred Trust. I am alone now — the last one left. We were keepers of an abomination that was created ages ago. A Portrait. The Sufletul Mortii, Romanian for Soul Eater. It's a portrait of evil. No! It's a portrait that is the very essence of evil.
>
> Our order was created to be caretakers of the portrait. We dedicated our lives to this sole purpose. We believed that had we kept the Sufletul Mortii locked away and hidden, that it would keep the world safe. We were mistaken. Nothing can keep the world safe as long as there are admirers to behold its sick and wicked beauty.
>
> It wasn't long after we secured the portrait that things began to go awry. The first to succumb to the portrait's evil was Brother Thaddeus. He heard noises in the cellar and fearing mice, went to investigate. When the rest of us arrived, we were horrified. All that was left of him was his skeletal remains on the floor.
>
> The next to fall prey was Brother Andrew.
>
> He performed an exorcism on the portrait, believing this would rid it of its evil. In the middle of the exorcism, we heard a loud crash. The portrait had fallen on him. The ornately detailed metal frame landed on him and broke his neck.
>
> When we lifted the portrait off of him, Brother Edward and Brother Stuart cut their hands on the frame very badly. Both later developed some kind of blood infection and died after a lengthy and painful illness.
>
> We long debated what to do about this evil. Brother Paul suggested that we bury it, but it was decided that it was too dangerous to touch. It had been buried before in its history and always seemed to quite literally resurface.
>
> It seemed that any course of action we took towards the portrait resulted in some sort of repercussion that ended in

death. We kept it hidden away, locked up, until we could come to a conclusion on the matter.

Others here also succumbed to the wickedness of the portrait. Brother Mattias suffered a heart attack after gazing at it for lengthy periods of time. Father Michael began to pound on the portrait in anger, until his hands were bloodied. His demise reminded me of the scene in Macbeth. When he couldn't wash the blood off his hands, he went insane. We found him hanging from a beam in his room.

Then it was Brother Clinton and Brother Paul. Brother Clinton attempted to burn the portrait with a torch, and I swear it was the Devil's breath that blew, setting him aflame. We stood in horror as he burned to death.

Brother Paul finally took an axe to the portrait several times. After having finished, he turned his back for a moment, and something from the portrait reached out and decapitated him.

Eventually thirteen of us would die over the years. After each death, the portrait seemed more vivid and powerful. Unfortunately, those in the church that knew of our oath had passed on, and so we were forgotten.

Finally there was only me. The seriousness of the task kept me going all of these years. I knew it was too important to not continue. It was my duty. I had sworn an oath to God.

In my loneliness, especially on dark and chilly nights, I could feel and hear the portrait call out to me. Chiding me. Teasing me. It knew I was alone.

But I remained strong. I avoided the portrait room. It was the only way to stay safe and stay alive. Yet I grew to feeling ill as of late.

One day, just after my evening prayers, during a particularly bad storm, I thought I heard a crash. I grabbed this book and headed back to its room. As I reached for the door, it opened by itself.

The portrait, the Sufletul Mortii, was waiting for me.

I entered, sitting down in a chair at the back of the room. While I didn't stare directly at the portrait, I knew it was coming for me. Wanting me. Wanting me like a predator watching its prey.

I also realized I was dying. My time here was ending. I started to recite the prayers for exorcism, but my pain was too great and I had to stop. I think I fainted. I woke up *hours later, weaker than before. I performed my last rites, then I began to write this warning.*

The portrait is alive. The darkness is come for me. I no longer have the strength to fight it. It is coming...It's —

I didn't know what to think. Maybe these were the delusions of an old and lonely man? Yet I knew better. I didn't know what to believe. I could only go by what I had witnessed thus far. Deep down, though, I knew it to be true. It was all so unbelievable to comprehend.

A loud crash brought me out of my reverie.

Constance was missing.

I headed off to find her. The door to the portrait room was open. I dreaded entering but did without hesitation.

Instantly, I was greeted by a sight of pure revulsion.

The portrait had fallen on Peter, crushing him. His face was still frozen in terror.

I looked closely along the frame of the portrait. The metal was very sharp in the more ornate spots. It reminded me of a rose with its thorns, and I wondered if it had been deliberate in design. Remembering Brother Frederick's warning, I looked for something to lift the portrait off of Peter, fearing to touch it.

Constance let out a scream and then began to cry. I stood there, holding her, trying to calm and reassure her, but I was having little effect.

We left the portrait room, closing the door behind us. I started to look around for something that could help lift the portrait and found nothing. I hated to leave him like that, but I didn't want to touch that portrait, especially after what I had just read.

Now there was just the two of us.

Constance sat down in the corner and began to weep. We held each other, trying to comfort one another; baffled that less than a few hours before, we were a simple group of friends trekking through Europe. Soon she began kissing me and before I knew it we were in throws of passion, making love. We had momentarily forgotten about the portrait, about Peter and Veronica.

We slept. I don't know for how long, but I woke up alone. The sanctuary felt icy and cold.

Constance was nowhere to be found. It was night, and the worst of the storm had moved off in the distance.

Then I thought I heard something.

Listening, my ears heard some kind of deep, hoarse laughter.

I grabbed an oil lamp and headed towards the portrait room. I was scared, but wanted to find Constance. I wanted to find her and get the hell out of this cursed place.

As I got closer, I could hear voices and faint, yet eerie music.

I stopped at the door, not wanting to proceed but knowing I had no choice.

Quickly, I opened the door. Much to my surprise, the portrait was back on the wall. Peter's body was still on the floor.

There, being pulled into the portrait by some dark entity, was Constance. I knew she had been seduced by the evil from within it. I screamed and threw the oil lamp at the *Sufletul Mortii*, now fully understanding its meaning.

Fire broke out when the lamp crashed and exploded on the wall, erupting the room in flames.

I ran out of there as the fire began to spread throughout the old monastery. I could hear screams and moans, intermingled with the hoarse laughter coming from the portrait.

I made my way out of the monastery into the rain, and down the road running in to the blackened evening. I found my way to a nearby town where I collapsed and was taken to the hospital.

For all anyone knew, my companions and I sought refuge overnight at the old monastery when an oil lamp fell over; causing the fire that killed my friends. When I recovered, I went home, where I kept my secret.

That was over twenty years ago.

I had hoped the oil lamp destroyed the *Sufletul Mortii* and for years believed that it had. Then one day I noticed an auction at Christie's dealing with an art auction of rarely seen portraits and paintings, and felt compelled to attend.

I saw Constance—her Doppelganger, albeit older—reminding me that the real Constance had been pulled into the portrait. Her double was affixing a portrait to an easel for display.

A chill went up my spine.

It was the first time I saw the portrait in over twenty years.

I was sure the portrait knew I was there. I was disturbed to discover that an anonymous benefactor spent millions purchasing the *Sufletul Mortii* for a record price. Its wicked beauty was beheld by many that day, and it ensnared a new victim.

The portrait was back and it brought with it all of the evil that had been hidden from the world for so long.

And I knew it was going to make up for lost time.

Tom Sawyer *began his professional writing career as a sports and features reporter for the* Pontiac-Waterford Times *in 1978 at age seventeen. Since then, he has gone on to write for a number of papers that include the* Oakland Press, The Daily Tribune, The Reminder Newspapers, *and* The Bay City Times. *He's written several short stories and the novel* The Lighthouse. *His newest novel* Firesale *is available from Infinity Publishing.*

Vanity

Kristi Petersen Schoonover

Mirror, mirror on the wall was a relative of mine. I did not admit that with shame; rather, I was proud to boast of a many-shadowed history on countless chateau walls, proud to herald that I had bolstered the images of a variety of intriguing women. Whether robust or delicate, voluptuous or reedy, withering or ripening—I showed each she was beautiful. I engaged my subjects; I was certain the typical fate of silvering and aging, which happens to mirrors from staring endlessly at the same image without reaction, would never happen to me.

It was a chilly October day, my prior owner Mary's estate sale. There had not been much in my vision all afternoon save for dappling sun and leaves. And then, a sweet, fair face appeared. She had a pretty pink pock mark below the outer corner of one eye; I had seen birthmarks like it, but never there. It sat like a painted rose on white china, and drew me into her dark eyes.

A female voice: "Cassie? We should think about leaving."

My admirer did not look back over her shoulder in the direction from which the voice had come. Instead, she cocked her head to the left, and to the right. She mussed her hair.

I swelled up to reflect her. I rounded her chin, blushed her cheeks.

She gave me a faint smile. "I've decided. This mirror would be stunning in my bedroom, don't you think?"

Cassie bought me for less than I was worth, but I was not insulted; she was such a fine creature, I would have begged to be taken home with her for free had she not been willing to pay. She lifted me with gentle hands, threw a dust-and-cat-hair-clouded blanket over me, and put me into the trunk, where I lay in darkness and felt the bumps in the road. I anxiously waited for the arrival at her home. I wanted to study everything she owned. I wanted to know her.

✠

Every woman in my life had a love for someone; if what I reflected when each looked into me would have an effect on attaining her wildest dreams, I would give it, even if it meant I might lose her — in my earliest memory, I was frequently passed to a different owner if my current one wed. I had come to expect it; it was my fate to love, and to lose.

When I arrived at Cassie's, for the first time, I dreaded that day. For Cassie beheld me in ways that none before her had. She scrutinized me closely, seemed to peer through me, turning this way and that, touching her legs, her arms, her flesh, asking me if I thought she was beautiful. Of course she was, even surpassing the white roses for which she had a passion — and there was no part of her body on which they weren't in bloom. She had art on her shoulder, back, and ankle; she had metal ones which entwined and grew up the outer lobe of her ear; she even had them on her shopping hat, the one I had heard her tell her friend her lover Dan had bought her in a fashionable sea-side shop.

Dan. On and on she talked of him, at first, never in front of me — always with other females, always from somewhere else in the house. Dan was a painter, and she would babble with excitement about how she was going to be his subject. "With a little more work, of course," I'd heard her say on a few occasions, sometimes when I could surmise from the lilt in her voice that she had been imbibing. On those nights, she would look into me even more deeply, and I would respond and reflect her loveliness, add a little paunch to her cheeks if they looked slightly gaunt, brush a bit of flesh on her inner arms to match what I had seen on her that first day she'd lifted me from the grass.

And then one night, she did not just look into me.

She *touched* me, at the point where my gaze met her thighs.

There was a flood of something as I had never felt, like the sound of sand in an hourglass, to which I had been close enough once to hear, only this was a feeling, not a sound, and then all went black.

For one moment, I was…I could not *see!*

"Not enough," she whispered. "I am not beautiful enough to be part of his canvas. I must be thinner."

I was shocked back to vision. She was Renaissance, as the women in the paper photo hanging over her bed reminded me they were, roun-

ded and luminescent, lush and enveloping and certainly not fat, and I
adored her just that way, every line and shade: the gentle, graceful collarbone, the fleshy swell of her stomach, even when a small bulge rose
above her waistband, the breasts, one more angular than its mate, the
legs which met in four out of five places.

I couldn't bear to have her think that. To show her that I would wor-
ship her regardless, I daubed extra flesh on her belly, padded a curve
on her thigh, accentuated the pouch beneath her chin. I waited for her
to smile, as she had that day on the lawn.

But instead her eyes narrowed, and she fled from the room.

The next dawning she stood before me in a sheer gown, posing: Forward, backward, side, poking her stomach, caressing her knees, pressing her collarbone, wrapping fingers around her wrist, twisting her
rings. Then she would touch me in those same places, and I would go
blind for a second and then not, blind and then not, and always when
I was not I would embellish her, a little curve here, a small rise there.

"We will make this perfect," she said, and then she left, and I could
barely stand the anticipation of her return so I could know what she
meant.

She arrived harboring a brown bag, and sat in front of me. "This will
work," she said, and spilled the bag's contents on the floor. There
were aqua boxes and red boxes and bottles of green glass. "I will be a
sketch instead of charcoal, if that is what he wants so he can love me,
so he can draw me." She ripped into the red box with savage delight,
opened the small bottle inside, filled her palm with several red pills,
and slapped them into her yawing mouth.

It became ritual. She took the pills, she pulled herself into a floun-
cing red dress; she twisted her hair into a clip crowned with white
roses. She stood before me, turned, cocked her arm, twirled. I
rendered flesh upon her each time; to show her my love for her was
purer than Dan's, to show her my love was all she would ever need.

"Not enough," she said.

Her bones began to show. Dresses she filled hung off her body. The
meeting places in her legs shrank from each other; her knees whittled
to bas-relief. The more she looked into me, the angrier she seemed to
become, and so I worked even harder to flesh her out, and the amount
I was required to add each instance grew. I expended such energy that
sometimes, in the shadows when the room was dark and she was in
bed, I hardly had energy to watch over her.

Once, she stopped mid-twirl, and her eyes clouded with misery. "This is not going as fast as it needs to."

That was the beginning of the small chocolates from the aqua box and the thirsty consumption of the liquid in the green bottles; some dawnings now were full of the distant noises of sickness—a sound I knew all too well from having been set upon the walls of water closets before. Harder I worked to show my love.

I mourned her former self. I wanted to see her as she was the first day she bought me, the way I had seen her when she gazed into me, the way I had seen her that magic night when her fingers had touched me and quickened my silver. I did not reflect her as she was, because I could not bear to look at her as she was. I fleshed up her collarbone so the outlining shadows disappeared; I swelled her shriveling breasts. When sometimes it was difficult to restore her, I looked to her armoire for inspiration, for there were images there: Cassie executing an arabesque; Cassie in her white rose hat; Cassie, her arms around a man whom I hoped was not Dan but suspected otherwise.

The more like a stick she became, the more I brush-stroked her body, filled her clothes. I waited for her to dispose of Dan's image, but she wouldn't, which meant I restored her further, so I could impress upon her even more clearly that I loved her the way she had been—I was not like Dan, and yet *still* she did not acknowledge. Each day it was anger upon anger. She stood before me; she wept and cursed. And there was nothing I could do to comfort her except to add flesh upon her bones and wait for her to see me.

One dawning, when the bedroom walls were brighter than usual because of the newly-fallen snow outside the French doors, she stared at me with burning hate, contempt in her eyes. "I hate you," she murmured, low, threatening. "You are worthless. You are evil, and you deserve nothing."

How could she say this to me? All I had wanted to do was love her; all I had given her was love; all I had wanted was her love in return because Dan, the lover, he was not right for her. I was the only thing she needed to love, and we would dwell in her room of the white roses forever; we were meant to be as one. It was fate; my final home was to be with her.

Mirrors, we have horror stories. That there is fire in the home and we crack in the heat; that there are arguments between lovers and we are accidentally struck with a candlestick, a lamp, an ashtray; that we are carelessly anchored and slip from the wall. These are terrible ways to be disfigured, for certain. But there is another way, one that is disrespected for it is considered most selfish: a self-inflicted shattering. It is an extreme thing, never to be practiced except in excruciating situations, and it is a serious undertaking. It is a commitment one makes to the mutilation, and, perhaps, permanent destruction, of oneself, for it means that one believes nothing will be more painful than what one is watching.

In that moment, I shattered, and hundreds of incidents many shadows, many dawnings, many women ago returned to me, all at once: the shriek/wail of one suddenly widowed owner; the heat of a too-close candle of another during something called a séance; the smell of another giving birth in a straw bed. Only these were all inside me, all at once, and overwhelming, and I had expected to go momentarily blind but I did not and instead watched Cassie as my surface cracked and split.

In the after, she glowered at me and I wondered what she saw, for all I could see of her through the shatter was disjointed, disconnected, dismembered, like the painting that had hung across from me in my last owner Mary's dining room, the one she had bragged to her dinner guests was a "real Picasso."

"You can't do this to me anymore!" She thrust her hands over her ears. "I won't listen to you, I won't!"

She fled from the room, and I heard commotion from below, clashing and crashing and yes, even breaking glass. And then she returned, and stood before me, and she took out a long, silver object.

A carving knife. I had seen one in Mary's dining room. It was for slicing meats, and…

…she pressed the blade against her wrists.

I think I screamed. I am not sure.

Eventually, she went still, and there was no sound, no nothing. Her vacant eyes stared into mine. She was so close to me, I could not feel any fog on me from her breath. I wanted to get down off the wall and shake her! Make her look at me! Make her see me! But I could not. All I could do was press forth a piece of my backing to let loose a shard. It fell to the carpet with a *tink-thud*.

Many shadows passed, and then, it all ended with bugs. At first, there was only one, in the layer of dust that had formed on the antique trunk at the foot of the bed. Then another bug joined him, and another, and they made paisley patterns on her nose and eyes, colliding and bouncing off one another until a teeming quilt of them thrummed over her body.

Through the shatter, I watched her melt away.

Kristi Petersen Schoonover's *fiction has appeared in* The Adirondack Review, Barbaric Yawp, Full of Crow Fiction Quarterly, Macabre Cadaver, Morpheus Tales, New Witch, The Smoking Poet, Toasted Cheese, *and others, including several anthologies. She holds an MFA in Creative Writing from Goddard College, is the recipient of two Norman Mailer Writers Colony Winter Residencies, and is an editor for* Read Short Fiction. *Her recent book,* Skeletons in the Swimmin' Hole—Tales from Haunted Disney World, *is a collection of ghost stories set in Disney Parks, and her novel,* Bad Apple, *is forthcoming from Vagabondage Press Books in November, 2011.*

The Mumbai Malaise

SP Hampton, Sr.

A deafening chorus of high pitched chirping echoed through the blackness and gave way to a frantic fluttering of wings as if a great host of sparrows took flight. The chirping mingled with the beating of wings became a savage rhythmic music that became a haunting unearthly music accompanied by a sensual feminine voice that penetrated the soul with an incalculable sadness. The music grew louder and louder…

✠

"Oscar?"

Oscar Bailey's eyes snapped open; an involuntary shudder ran through him as the music faded. He sat up in the oversized, cushioned conference table chair and rubbed his forehead.

"Sorry. I haven't been sleeping well lately."

"None of us have," replied his analytical Assistant Director Dr. Anatoli Sokolov, as he clasped his hands together as if about to pray, above the folders spread before him.

"Amen to that," added Dr. Matthew Peters, Information Technology & Communications Director.

"So," Oscar summed up the hours long meeting in his richly decorated office, "we are alone."

"Very much so," Anatoli said. "The last supply ships will enter orbit in three days time. They will be the last for the foreseeable future."

"How about forever?" Matthew responded in a barely controlled voice. "Shanghai has fallen silent. Mumbai, Moscow, Mexico City, New York City, London, and Cairo, have all gone silent."

"We are alone," Oscar repeated. He still heard the frantic fluttering of the sparrows; if God knew of the death of even one sparrow, maybe He was overwhelmed by the death of an entire world of sparrows. How else to explain His disappearance? "How is everyone responding?"

"Depression," Anatoli shrugged.

"An overwhelming sense of doom and gloom among some, denial among others," said Matthew as he gave his detached, analytical colleague an irritated look. "I wouldn't rule out suicides in the near future."

"Possible," Anatoli said, "however please leave that analysis to me. Your forte is Information Technology and Communications."

"And you're an astronomer!"

"Gentlemen," Oscar held up a weary hand. "We cannot escape reality. Our self-imposed quarantine is in place. It's unnecessary because there are no more visitors, nonetheless…. We have contingency plans that include food and supply rationing. We'll expand the hydroponic gardens. Waste recycling and water and oxygen mining will keep us going indefinitely. As long as the sun doesn't go nova, our solar panel arrays will keep the station powered." He looked at his compatriots. "The Earth dies. We live. Now, we have to do something to provide a distraction to the staff so that everyone can emotionally reset."

"Like what?" Matthew frowned.

Anatoli gave Oscar a puzzled look.

"I was watching the news before I fell asleep last night," Oscar said. "I saw a concert in Rio de Janeiro by that new entertainer who's taken the world by storm in the past few years. Lady Gaia. 'The Cleansing of the World Tour', she calls it."

"A concert?" Anatoli raised his eyebrows. Matthew's mouth dropped open.

"We decorate the Amphitheatre and hold a party. We make available half of our alcohol stock, provide appetizers, and a buffet meal. It will be a party to take people's mind off of the current situation. And it will be a celebration of our survival."

"I'm not sure this is the wisest course of action," Anatoli said.

"It's stupid. It's like Nero fiddling while Rome burns," Matthew growled.

"Nonetheless, it's what we'll do," Oscar responded with his customary stubbornness and self-assurance. Such an attitude had gotten him far in life, though it also made many enemies. "I believe we still have a genuine artist here?"

Matthew nodded. "Nikita Sharma. She's from northern India, in the Himalayas."

"Good. Have her decorate the Amphitheatre. She's to have whatever she needs."

"Are you certain?" Anatoli asked.

"Yes. Let's make it happen, gentlemen." Oscar signaled the end of the meeting by scooping up the file folders on the table.

Afterwards he sat at his desk and clicked on the earth icon on his computer screen. The cloudy blue-green world hung suspended against the velvet blackness of space, just above the nearby brown-gray mountain range on the horizon. He was reminded of a 20th century Apollo 8 photograph entitled, "Earthrise." So much had changed since mankind's first fledgling steps into space.

A small space station orbited Earth, robot probes roamed Mars and solar sail powered robot spacecraft were speeding on their way out of the solar system. But mankind's crowning achievement was the five year-old Lunar Scientific Research Station located in a large meteorite crater in the Lunar Highlands. It was a flimsy toehold protected by a roof of steel plates supported by medieval style arches and pillars. Inside the crater metal walkways connected the various prefabricated administrative, scientific, and living quarters buildings — actually, curved-roof Quonset huts. Nearby, also built underground, was a variety of buildings whose functions were necessary for the survival of the research station.

A thousand men and women inhabited the Station. More than two hundred professions were represented — from scientists to plumbers and miners. Even stone masons, sculptors, and painters.

Over them all was Oscar Bailey, a portly, successful lawyer and a Federal Appeals Court Justice. Upon learning of the pending establishment of the station he maneuvered his way into becoming the Director. He was the perfect match — after all, what the Station needed more than anything was someone with a logical mind, the skill to meld a diverse population into a team, and the ability to prioritize near-term and long-term goals.

It was his intent that the Station be more than a research station — due to the grave environmental challenges and growing plagues on Earth, it would become a last haven for the survival of mankind.

Thus, Oscar ruled the station like it was his personal fiefdom, and in many ways it was.

He clicked on another icon and Earth filled the screen. The clouds were dusty white and the oceans a deep blue. Asia was daylight bright, while the night side of the world was blacker, for there were far fewer cities than before. Some cities, however, flickered with the glow of raging fires. He clicked the screen for a closer image. The brown mountain ranges of Tibet gave way to lush green valleys and plains. The snow and glaciers in the Himalayas reminded him of thin, jagged sprays of ice across a car windshield on frosty mornings.

Oscar thought he detected a brownish haze to the images—it wouldn't surprise him if there was. Funeral pyres consumed a lot of wood—but was there enough wood in the world to burn all of the dead?

The Mumbai Malaise was such a mundane name for something that threatened the existence of humanity. Whatever it was, it was birthed among the unwashed millions in the slums of Mumbai, and spread like wildfire throughout the city, India, and across the world. The infected developed an agonizing headache, fever, and collapsed in delirium. As they thrashed about, blood flowed from every orifice including old, formerly healed wounds.

In spite of quarantines it found even the most remote villages and towns. The world ran out of coffins and the dead were burned on wood pyres and within their homes. When the living became too afraid to approach the dead and dying, they were left in the streets. Roving flamethrower teams and 'Molotov cocktail teams' using the ubiquitous rag burning glass bottles of gasoline, set fire to the dead where they fell. Whenever animals, even family dogs, had feasted on the dead, they were killed and burned. Not all bodies were found, and perhaps the rotting corpses released deadly fumes wafted away by the winds.

Science had no answer for such a rapidly moving pestilence; a disease that killed so quickly normally "burned itself out" because it killed the host faster than it could spread. Among the many doomsday cults that sprang up was the belief that Earth was a living being, and it was finally cleansing itself of the fatal parasite that was mankind.

The only proven islands of immunity were the orbiting space station and the moon station.

Oscar set the communications icon for scan, settled back and watched Earth. The office filled with bursts of static, frantic voices, and bits of recognizable conversations. He stiffened as he realized the scratchy static resembled the massive fluttering of wings intermingled with the sad cries of frightened sparrows. Behind the wild cacophony was the haunting music from his dream.

A tear gathered in the corner of his eye and trickled down his cheek.

✠

"Cheers," Oscar forcefully put a beer in Matthew's hand and clinked their bottles together. The small man looked confused. "Well?"

"Cheers," Matthew answered quietly.

Throngs of people filled the floor of the amphitheatre, spilled across the stage, and up into the seats. Bluish smoke from barbeque stands drifted through the air, and loud music blared from speakers. Though the people laughed, sang, danced, ate and drank, the gaiety had a sense of artificial desperation about it.

"Set the example for our people," Oscar ordered as he draped a friendly arm around Matthew's shoulders and guided him toward a buffet table overflowing with steaks and french fries. "Put on a happy face."

"All of the cities are silent now."

"Yes. It's not surprising considering that satellite communications networks require highly trained technicians in order to operate. I really doubt if everyone on Earth is dead. However, thank you." Anatoli emerged from a bluish haze, beer in hand though the somber look on his face hadn't changed from their meeting a few days before.

"Cheers," Oscar smiled and clinked his bottle against Anatoli's.

"The supply ships arrived in orbit a few hours ago."

"Good, good. We'll unload them in a couple of days."

Anatoli looked at the gathered crowd, the buffet tables, and the kitchen staff and volunteers hurrying back and forth with food and drink.

"This is using up a fifth of food reserves. Especially the meats."

"All for a good purpose, I assure you," Oscar clapped Anatoli on the shoulder. He looked at the decorated amphitheatre, especially the lengths of colored crinkle paper that hung from the steel roof and whose dangling ends almost touched the heads of the celebrants. The paper was clustered so that in the center it reminded one of a blue waterfall, while on the flanks clusters of brown and gray recalled mountain slopes, and the green paper at the ends recalled forests. Above all, and dangling from roof beam to roof beam, was yards of black crinkle paper along which, at various intervals, dangled small papier-mâché balls painted yellow to recall the stars. Scattered around the amphitheatre and up the steps were luminaries, small paper bags filled with moon dust in which a lit candle burned. "Nikita did a good job, didn't she? We need to reward her."

"Yes," Anatoli nodded.

"This is so wrong," Matthew shook his head as he gulped his beer. "I'm going to get drunk just so I can forget all this crap."

"Get drunk if you want but change your attitude," Oscar growled and pulled the man closer by his shirt. "Tonight everyone resets their attitude so we can keep going and survive."

"We party while the world dies."

"Yes."

"Yes sir, boss," Matthew jerked free and wandered away.

"If he wasn't the expert among us," Oscar began, and then said, "we need to train another IT&C expert as soon as possible."

"If you want to thank Nikita, she's sitting at the top of the amphitheatre," Anatoli changed the subject and pointed.

"Yes, thank you." Oscar grabbed a spare beer and wound his way among the throng, many of whom were dancing wildly and seductively, up the wooden steps. As a result of his determination not to be shackled by a penny pinching, unimaginative bureaucracy, especially in the face of disasters overtaking the world, the amphitheatre was the only structure in the crater that was beautiful and unnecessary.

It was set against the slope of the crater wall and was built like a classical Greek amphitheatre. The curved back wall was built of granite and wood; the bas-reliefs along the back wall were constructed from shattered basalt moon rocks, shaped and arranged like vertical Roman mosaics. The steps and seats were built of wood; the parodos, the walkway to the side of the amphitheater where actors entered, and the orchestra, or circular dancing space in front of the amphitheater, was paved with flagstone. Behind the orchestra was the stage, also of wood, and behind the stage was the skene, a wooden building the front of which was the decorated part of the set. Concerts and dances, as well as town hall meetings, were often held at the amphitheatre. Even when not in official use, it was a popular gathering place.

"Hello," he called as he approached a solitary young woman seated at the highest level. He held the beer out to her.

Nikita Sharma was a petite, dusky skinned woman with long black hair with red highlights. Her dark eyes were sad, her lips small and sensual.

"Hello." She eyed the bottle. "Thank you, but I don't drink."

"The more for me," Oscar replied cheerfully as he settled his bulk next to her. He glanced at the steel roof that felt uncomfortably close. "Wonderful decorating you did here. Wonderful."

"Thank you."

"Just as you did a magnificent job with the Amphitheatre as a whole."

She smiled. "My concept, though architects and laborers did all of the technical work and construction." Nikita looked at him. "Thank you for bringing everything we needed from Earth."

"Not a problem. I wanted something beautiful here, something to connect us with our home."

She studied the crowded amphitheatre. "It will outlive us too, just like the buildings and sculptures of ancient cultures outlived their creators."

Oscar gave her a quizzical look. "Yes. I suppose so. It's strange you would mention that. You're part Greek, and...?"

"My mother is Greek and my father is from India."

"Yes, of course. Both are wonderful countries."

"I was raised in both. I love the ancient feel of Greece, and the even more ancient feel of northern India, where I was born. Greece is so beautiful and alive in the spring when the olive groves are in bloom. The Himalayas are so beautiful, especially at sunrise and sunset. There's nothing like winter there, when the snows are deep, and cedar wood is burning in the fireplace. I miss all of it." She glanced at him. "I'm sorry, I didn't mean to go on like that."

"That's quite all right." He finished his beer and opened the second. "I've been thinking of how to reward you." She looked at him. "I was thinking of extra food rations, or extra alcohol rations. Money won't be of any use anymore. But, as the Director of this station, I'm sure we can work something out that will be mutually beneficial to the both of us."

She returned his overly friendly smile with a cautious look. Her dark eyes gave no hint of what she was thinking. He finally turned away and took another drink of his beer.

He froze as within the roar of the crowd he thought he heard the fluttering of wings. Though he knew it was ridiculous, he scanned the amphitheatre, the space between the thick roof supports, and the Quonset huts and walkways. The strong overhead lights hanging from the roof created pools of light interspersed with dark shadows.

Oscar saw half a dozen men running out of the amphitheatre and onto the walkways. They weren't revelers; there was an urgent sense of purpose to their action.

He glanced at Nikita but wasn't sure what to say. He looked in the direction the men ran.

"I suppose I should thank you for bringing me here."

"What?"

"You brought me here after the Station was built. You told me that you wanted something beautiful here. I guess it was a stroke of luck, or fate, that I came to be here. I mean, while so many were dying on Earth. Sometimes I feel guilty."

"There's no need to feel guilty. And I'm glad that you're here."

"Thank you." She looked at him again, her lips pressed together.

"Yes?"

"Ultimately, it may not matter."

Oscar frowned. He saw more men running out of the amphitheatre. The ceiling lights flickered and several exploded in bright sparks. The sound system hissed and crackled. For a moment it seemed frantic voices screamed and pleaded through the static. The partygoers fell silent.

"Excuse me." Though being such a portly man Oscar could move fast when he needed to. He hurried down to the orchestra. The speaker static continued to hiss and crackle so that many people held their hands over their ears. Sometimes the static screeched like high pitch chirps or fluttered like the beating of wings. More ceiling lights exploded in showers of sparks. A frightened murmur ran through the crowd.

Faint musical notes whispered through the static, growing stronger until the music displaced the static. It was a strange unworldly music that was ancient before mankind's earliest ancestor first crawled onto land. It was a dirge that sang of creation and destruction, a music that chilled the soul and brought sadness to the heart. It was the music of Earth that was carried across the world by winds that had always been and always would be.

It was a music that Oscar knew but couldn't place.

"Shut that off," Anatoli appeared through the barbeque smoke and pointed at the DJ. "Shut it off!"

A dark figure appeared from behind a Quonset hut.

"I've tried," the DJ shrugged helplessly.

"Get the Communications Center," Oscar ordered. "Have them shut everything down."

"This is Dr. Sokolov," Anatoli spoke into his hand-held transmitter. "This is Dr. Sokolov. Come in."

The figure moved with an unhurried grace from one pool of light to another, and a feminine voice rose in a long, high pitched solo. More lights exploded. Oscar made out the dark form of a woman shrouded in red. The crowd turned toward the figure.

"Who the hell is that?" He demanded.

"This is Dr. Sokolov! Come in!"

The music grew louder. The figure disappeared behind the skene. The crowd drew away from the stage and the skene, and into the seats of the amphitheatre, or spilled along the parodos.

"They're not answering," Anatoli gave up.

"You two, get over to the Communications Center, shut everything down," Oscar pointed at a pair of women. They disappeared at a run.

The haunting music was louder and called to the soul and heart. It sang of what everyone knew but none wanted to admit. A woman stepped from between the curtains that draped the front of the skene. An uneasy murmur raced through the crowd. Oscar's eyes widened. More lights exploded.

Lady Gaia stood before them wrapped within a red silken shroud. She gazed out over the cowering crowd.

"Where the hell did she come from?" Oscar snapped at Anatoli over the music that came from everywhere within the crater. He looked around wildly. "Who broke quarantine? Who brought her here? Where the hell's Matthew?"

The shroud dropped around her red toe-nailed feet. A narrow red silk apron dangled from a golden waist chain, she wore a short red silk sleeveless top, and a royal blue silk sash around her waist. Gold ankle bracelets sparkled in the gloom.

"Security, get security to the stage," Anatoli radioed.

"Why the hell haven't they shut down communications?" Oscar yelled.

Lady Gaia spread her arms wide as if to embrace the crowd. People gasped as large red feathered wings unfurled behind her. She suddenly crouched with outspread arms and spun her head so that her long blonde and purple ponytail spun through the air above her. She moved in time with the music; she was the music that was filled with energy and even a joyful exuberance within such a soul crushing time. She flung her head back as if to gaze through the steel roof above, at the distant Earth. Her voice was beautiful, wild, and sensual.

"Security, answer me!" Anatoli shouted.

Lady Gaia spun so effortlessly that she was almost a blur before she dropped to one knee, supporting herself with a red finger nailed hand on the wooden stage. The red wings spread and closed as if in time to her breath.

She lifted her head and gazed at Oscar and Anatoli. Her obsidian eyes, highlighted with red eyeliner that angled outward to a point like ancient Egyptian eye makeup, sparkled with inhuman life. The back of her hand and her arm were decorated in unknown symbols of black henna.

Oscar staggered backwards before the power of the inhuman look.

She leaped gracefully into the air, and danced again; this time her sensual movements were more stylized as if she were performing a ceremony.

"Stop her!" Anatoli gave him a confused look in response. The music softened to match Lady Gaia's movements. "Dammit to hell! I'll stop her!"

"Matthew, where the hell are you?" Anatoli barked into his transmitter.

Oscar charged up the steps onto the stage. Lady Gaia spun again with arms held above her head. He grabbed her by the shoulders. Her flesh was hot and sweaty to the touch, and her black eyes bored into him. She gently placed a hand against his cheek. Her feathery red wings folded gracefully around them.

He cried out, grabbed his head and staggered backwards but the wings held him fast. The air was hot and heavy and suffocating within the embrace of her feathery soft wings. Lady Gaia smiled and placed her other hand on his other cheek. He tried to scream but only managed a choked gurgle. Oscar sagged and, as everything spun around him, he heard the beating of wings and the frightened cries of the sparrows. The feathery wings parted and he collapsed onto his side on the stage.

"Oh my God," Anatoli whispered. Everything analytical fled screaming into the darkness leaving only a frightened shell that trembled as Lady Gaia turned her obsidian eyes upon him. Ceiling lights exploded and a growing gloom flowed throughout the crater. The crowd erupted into screams, shouted pleas, and prayers, and scattered wildly. Already people grasped their throats or heads, staggered, and collapsed.

Howling like a small child, Anatoli ran around the stage and past the skene. His shoes kicked up puffs of moon dust that smelled so much like ash from a fireplace. He leaped onto the walkway and disappeared among the warren of Quonset huts.

There had to be an escape. Everything couldn't end with being trapped like a rat in a maze.

He stumbled over a body and plunged onto the crater floor. Choking in the moon dust he froze as he saw Matthew sprawled on his back, head hanging limply, bloody eyes staring at him blankly.

"Oh no, no, oh no," Anatoli shook his head and crawled backwards away from the body. He backed into something and looked up.

Lady Gaia leaned over him and smiled. Her long blonde and purple hair caressed his face. Her red wings unfurled and draped across him as if to shelter him, or trap him. Anatoli screamed as his head throbbed painfully and he rolled in the dust until he curled up in a fetal position and became motionless.

The music became faster and Lady Gaia sauntered a few short steps down the walkway, her red feathery wings stretched wide, before she danced again. Her voice and body melded with the unearthly music, and became a timeless rhythm of Earth that always had been and always would be.

SS Hampton, Sr. *is a full blood Choctaw of the Choctaw Nation of Oklahoma. He is a divorced grandfather to 12 grandchildren, a published photographer and photojournalist, and a veteran of Operations Noble Eagle and Iraqi Freedom. His fiction writings have appeared in* Melange Books, Horror Bound Magazine, Ruthie's Club, *and* Lucrezia Magazine, *among others. He has an anthology of his short stories forthcoming in 2012 from* Melange Books; *he has a short story appearing in 2011 in another anthology from* Melange Books, *and a short story forthcoming in 2012 from* MuseItUp Publishing. *He currently resides in Las Vegas, Nevada.*

The Apprentice's Tale

Jennifer L. Gifford

When asked why I did it, revenge was the only motive that came to mind. I did not want to appear as someone who is deranged, babbling on irrationally, trying to prove my saneness to others. I did not want to appear as someone who uses the weakened condition of their mental capacity as an excuse for the crimes they have committed. The things that I have done seem minuscule to the punishment for which I will undoubtedly receive. I can honestly say that I have no fear about dying, only that when I do, I will have no place to go.

My twisted tale starts off much like any other. Up until that moment in which all common sense escaped me, I had led an average and ordinary life. I was an accounting apprentice for Farley and Beckett, one the oldest and more prestigious firms in all of London. It was a position that I had strove for, for nearly two years, and several dozen letters of inquiry, before being taken on as an apprentice. I was learning a trade from one of the best in his profession, though I was merely a gopher for his endless errands and chores. But I did not belittle myself to these subservient tasks for the measly salary itself, no, no. I studied him, copied his every movement, just waiting for the one moment in which all of my tutelage and observance would pay off.

You see my mentor, Charles Edwin Farley, a well known and prestigious man in the community, was more than a mere accountant. He was a genius. Equal parts charming, deceitful, and cleaver, the man knew what cards to play when it came to getting what he wants. His actions went beyond mere swindling and blackmail. Mister Farley, as only a few of his close friends ever dared call him by his name, and it was always Charles, never Charlie at that, was a magistrate of injustice. He took it upon himself to balance one vile act out with another. Mister Farley was a master chess player, and his players were his business and social colleagues who were mentally or financially inferior.

I envied him in many ways; and emulated him in nearly every aspect of my daily routine. He bought his suits and hats from Suttleby's on the Square, the finest clothier in England. While I could never dream to ever make such an extravagant purchase from them, I was able to obtain older, gently worn pieces from a second hand clothier near the small one room flat I rented in Wellington. I styled my hair in the short and clean cut manner as Mister Farley. I read from the same paper; I ate the same foods whenever I could afford them.

"You learn their secrets, and they'll scratch your back whenever you demand it of them, my boy," he would cackled, peering over the edge of silver spectacles as he wrote from the leather bound journal he kept. Oh, that blasted book! On more than one occasion I vowed that I would secretly read his memoir, those thoughts of a mad genius. Every occasion on which I displeased or angered him, he would take out that leather-bound journal with the gold faced edges and scribble furiously without relent.

This is where my life, my simple and ordinary and not bad in its entirety, took a turn for the worse. I became obsessed with my performance, always making sure that my figures were accurate and my records were neat and up-to-date. But there was always something, some meticulous detail in which he would seek out and convey it to those blank pages. That book mocked me. I'd watch his fountain pen dip into the ink well, tap the glass rim, and the anger would then pulse through my veins with such hatred that it took all my strength to control it.

And my obsession grew. I found myself constantly peering over my shoulder, wondering if I would find the old man glaring at me, picking apart the way I worked much like the way a vulture picks apart a carcass. On and on he would ramble about decimal points, percentage rates, interest compounded daily, long term liability, on and on until I thought my head would explode. In those last few months, as I walked along the cobbled streets out of the posh neighborhoods of London towards my humble dwelling, my head would throb with an unyielding pulsation. And the more he needled me, the more my concentration became unfocused.

Then one day he left the office so inexplicably that I had not realized his departure until his return. It was late in the month of October, when the winds were turning colder, announcing winter's approach. I remember looking out the small paned windows of the office, as a fine mist drizzled throughout the morning. I must have spent a few hours staring out the window, looking at the black gates with the ornately sculpted iron that surrounded the property. There were very few pass-ersby that morning, and we had no appointments. My mind started to wander as soon as I sat at my desk and began to work. The hard slam of the massive oak door startled me out of my reverie.

"Sir," I said to him, "This bitter wind and drizzle is not ideal travel-ing weather. If you need an errand made, or require something specif-ic, I would be most assuredly glad to take it upon myself to fetch it for you."

"You have become so slow witted as of late, Barnes." He always called me by last name, never my first, and never a Mister, either. To him, my existence was nothing more that the surname from which I had derived.

"Sir, I am," I stammered but he held up a hand to cut me off.

"For your information, Barnes, I have just returned from an errand to Bedforshire. It was something I had to do myself." Putting his cane into the umbrella stand, he reached inside his lapel pocket and handed me an envelope.

Trembling, I took the envelope, my fingers skimming over the soft feel of the luxurious card stock. My mind whirled at the thought of its contents. A raise? An invitation?

"Finish out the rest of the day, and first thing tomorrow morning, you're to be at the address listed inside. It's all there, black and white."

"Am I to assume that I will be setting up a new client tomorrow, Sir," I inquired, too nervous to do anything but clutch the letter furi-ously.

"No, your services here are terminated. You're expected at the of-fices of Beemer and Brown first thing. They'll explain when you get there," he smiled his crooked teeth grin at me.

The arrogant swine! The nerve to smile back at me, as if ripping away my future livelihood was some great accomplishment!

"But, Sir..." I managed to stammer. What could I possibly say to convince this madman that I was an earnest and worthy apprentice? "Sir, just look at all my accounts. They're neat, always up to date. I can assure you that..." But the old geezer cut me off, shaking his hands madly.

"Never you mind about that. I have seen what you consider quality work and it's all in here" he patted his leather journal that he had picked up from his desk, "and I do not wish to discuss this matter any further. That is all, Barnes."

And at that moment, at that very instance, my life changed forever. I snatched that leather-bound journal from his wrinkled hands and sung wildly, trying to focus all my anger toward him.

The first blow knocked him over, making his head hit the corner of the oak desk with a sickening crack. His eyes rolled up in his skull, and he gasped his last breath. But I was not content with the death of my mentor, oh no. I wanted to hurt him more, but the task seemed impossible for no life remained in his body.

I started shouting at him, "See what you made me do! Well I'll show you! Is this," I whacked him again, "up to your standards of quality?" With that, I began to beat him about the head with the corner of his journal several more times, until I was satisfied that not only did I batter his body but also his soul as well.

I sat back at his desk, smiling somewhat, much the way an artist admires his latest work. My hands trembled, but my eyes did not move from his corpse. And that's when I noticed an official letter, from the tyrant himself, sitting on the top of his desk ready to be mailed. Not giving a damn about what the old man might have thought, I snatched the paper and read it.

My hands shook and tears welled in my eyes. It was a letter of recognition to Beemer and Brown, praising my high standards of workmanship, and saying what a regret it will be to lose me, however Mister Farley stated that the personal accountant to a firm of well known and wealthy barristers was a far more prominent position than a mere apprentice.

Imagine my horror! The wretched tyrant, my beloved successor, had made a personal appearance to secure my new position. His bluntness at my termination was an attempt at humor. I was traumatized beyond belief.

With my head throbbing from all the crying I commenced to do, I laid my head upon the leather journal and sobbed uncontrollably. Yet as I lifted my head, I was once again filled with rage as I looked at the blood stained cover of the man's journal and wondered what vicious and ugly comments he had wrote about me. Carefully I opened it, to find sketches of houses, country scenes of little brooks with flowers along the bank, and several still life's of animals, mostly birds, perched upon long sinewy branches. Black and white sketches of the still life around him. Nothing, not one single word about me, my performance, not even a mention of the accounting firm itself.

So now I write the only entry in this journal, testifying to it as actual fact. I killed my mentor, Charles Farley. I shall live with the guilty shame until my maker banishes my blackened soul to roast in the fires of hell for all eternity.

Jennifer Gifford *has always had a fascination with the dark and humorous side of fiction. She hates creepy old dolls, spiders, and garden gnomes. Her work has been previously published in* Glutonlumps Chilling Tales, Demonminds Magazine, N.V.F.'s Halloween Anthology, And Soon…The Darkness, Mysteryauthors.com. M-Brane's Science Fiction Magazine *and* Breath and Shadow magazine. *She's been Assistant Editor of* Bête Noire Magazine *for nearly two years. She loves to read, to cook, and loves horror movies. Jennifer has been writing for almost two decades, and spends her time with her husband, writer A.W. Gifford, and their menagerie of animals.*

Until the Heart Betrays

A. W. Gifford

T *hump, thump, thump.*

That sound. That goddamn hollow sound of his cane on the hardwood floor. Not that he needs it. He can't walk, but it's his latest way of summoning me to do his bidding.

Thump, thump. "Lillian!" *Thump, thump, thump.*

This isn't the way things are supposed to be. I love him — or used to — and I thought he loved me. Yes, many people think I married him for his money, but that isn't the truth. That's why I didn't mind signing the pre-nup.

My friends thought I was stupid. Why, they said, if he loved me, did he think it necessary? I told them that his ex-wife cleaned him out and he was just trying to protect himself. Maybe that was the truth. More likely, I was just fooling myself.

We married when I was thirty-six and he was eighty-one. Some might call me a trophy wife: petite, blonde, with decent breasts. The pre-nup stipulated that, if we were to divorce, I would get ten million in a lump sum. That sounds like good money, but after years of putting up with his demands and mental abuse, it isn't enough. I want it all.

Thump, thump, thump!

I don't know how much more of this I can take. On some level I do still love him, but I'm getting older and I need time to enjoy all that money. This body and this face need some work, I'll admit, but the cheap bastard will never pay for it. He wouldn't pay for the breast enhancement I asked for a few years ago saying that my C cup was more than any woman needed.

Thump, thump. "Lillian!"

"Coming, dear!" I call. Patience is not one of his strong suits, but persistence on the other hand....

Over the last few weeks I've been giving him a daily dose of Thallium, but I think the poison just makes the bastard live longer.

Tonight, with dinner, he'll get a dose that I'm sure will kill him.

Thump, thump. "Lillian! I'm hungry." *Thump, thump, thump!*

I'll get him his damn dinner, then I'll break that cane over his bald, wrinkled head.

I walk to his study and stand in the doorway. This is his space and I'm not to violate it unless invited. He sees me and lays the cane across his lap. I just hate that thing. Slick ebony wood topped in a silver vulture's head with blue sapphires for eyes.

"Will you be coming to the dining room, honey? We can have dinner together."

"It's about damn time," he says. "Where the hell have you been? Didn't you hear me? I've been calling you for hours."

It was only a few minutes, but I guess when you're his age, every minute seems like an hour. "I'm sorry, dear, but I didn't hear you."

He sat in front of his television. At times I wondered if he could even the see the damn thing. But what do I care? As long as it keeps him out of my hair for most of the day he can watch the television until his eyes fall out.

"I'll take it here. I don't want to miss my shows."

I can't remember the last time we ate dinner—or any meal—together. He takes every meal in his study in front of that damn television.

"All right," I say. "I'll be right back."

I knew our private chef had already left for the evening, but before she did, she told me that dinner was in the oven. I go to the kitchen and pull the metal tray from the oven.

I was in luck this evening. Tonight's dinner consists of wild rice soup, roasted asparagus, mashed potatoes and a small beef fillet.

Separating my food from his, I reach into my pocket and pull out a small vile of the poison. I sprinkle a bit on top of the soup and stir it in making sure there are no clumps and sprinkle some more, on the asparagus and season the fillet with a generous dose.

Putting the bottle back into my pocket, I place his food on a silver serving tray and carry it into the study.

I don't need verbal permission to enter when I'm bringing his food. The cane is still across his lap and I feel those vulture's eyes following me as I enter. I set the tray on his desk and set up a folding tray in front of him. After I place his food down, he pats my arm. "Thank you," he says. "You're too good to me."

God dammit. This whole thing would be much easier if he was just an old bastard all the time.

"Why don't you taste the soup and let me know if it is warm enough for you."

He picks up the spoon, dips into the soup and takes a long slurp. Smacking his lips he says, "Oh, that's good. Thank you, Cookie."

A small part of me wants to take the soup and dump it, but once he uses that term of endearment—one I really hate—I decide to stand there for a moment and watch him eat. "Will there be anything else?"

"No, I think I'm good. I'll call you when I'm done."

I'm not sure how long it will take for the poison to finish him off. I'm hoping for that moment he will gag and grab his neck, but it never happens. Poisonings aren't like they are in the movies.

I walk back to the kitchen and eat my food standing at the counter. It's just too lonely to sit at the dining room table all by myself.

The evening gives way to the silence of his cane.

At nine, I go to his study door to see if he is dead. Most nights by this time, he would have summoned me to help him get ready for bed. Some nights he falls asleep in his chair and I just leave him there until he wakes. Tonight looks to be one of those nights. On the television, a lion is chasing an antelope; one animal killing another. His favorite thing to watch.

I stand in the doorway for a moment. The room is dark and all I can make out in the flickering light of the television is that he's slumped in his chair; the cursed cane lay across his lap, its eyes mocking me. I notice no movement from breathing, so I venture forth.

With years of him yelling at me for the most minor of infractions, I half-expect him to sit up and scream at me to get the hell out of his study, but he does none of that.

I kneel in front of him. No breathing that I can detect. I hold a finger under his nose and feel no movement of air.

It's over. I can't believe it. My heart pounds in my chest; part in exhilaration, part in fear.

Now, I can take him to bed and, in the morning, report his death.

Standing, I turn the television off.

"What the hell!" he screams and I jump.

"What are you doing in my study?"

"I was going to take you up to bed."

"Get out!" he screams and jabs me with his cane.

It hits me in my left side hard and I fall to the floor.

"Get out!" He jabs at me again.

I grab for the cane and manage to yank it out of his hands. Without thinking, I swing it towards him. The vulture's head connects with his left temple with a cracking *thud*.

At first, I think it's the cane breaking, but the old man falls out of his chair and I see blood pooling on the floor.

How the hell am I going to explain this? A ninety-three-year-old man found dead in his bed is easy to explain, but a ninety-three-year-old man lying on the floor in a pool of his own blood, not so much.

I complained on several occasions that we should have some live in help so I didn't have to be at his beck and call, but now I'm glad he never caved. With our chef already gone home and our cleaning crew not scheduled to come for a few days, I feel some relief. I have some time to work.

Though I hadn't planned it, earlier, I finish preparing my garden for a spring planting. There are no plants yet, just some freshly tilled soil. Digging a hole in my garden big enough to accommodate a person, a wheelchair and his wretched cane, doesn't appeal to me, but I know it has to be done and my garden is the perfect place for it. I like the idea of my flowers getting their nutrients off the bastard's body.

I walk out to my garden shed, but I don't turn on any of the lights. We don't have many neighbors, but the ones we do are close enough to notice a light.

Digging a hole is more work than I ever thought. When I finish, it's quite late and I'm tired. It looks like the first rays of morning are kissing the horizon. I just hope filling a hole is much easier.

I head back to the study; my blonde hair clings to my scalp in sweaty, dirty clumps. I feel disgusting. I take my shoes off outside so I don't drag any unnecessary dirt into the house. There is no need to make more work for myself.

I lock the wheels of his chair and lift him back into it. He's heavier than I thought he'd be, but I manage. I grab his cane, the vulture eyes stare back at me, taunting me; judging me.

We know what you've done, they seem to say.

I wheel him out to my garden and shove him into the hole—chair included. I drop the cane in as well, and the last I see of it are two beady blue orbs looking back at me as I drop, first the empty bottle of Thallium, then shovel full after shovel full of dirt back into the grave.

The sun has made its full rise over the horizon and I have the hole filled. My garden once again looks ready for the spring planting.

I retrace my steps, making sure that there are no wheel tracks or anything else that will betray me. I head back to the study and clean up the small pool of blood. I'm glad for hardwood floors now, as the clean up only takes a few minutes. I guess if anyone gets curious they might find some blood between the cracks, but I'm just too tired to worry about that right now. I'll do a better job in the morning.

After I shower, I fall into bed.

Thump, thump, thump.

I'm hearing that cane even in my dreams.

Thump, thump.

I awake just before four in the afternoon, disorientated. Then I hear the thumping again. It can't be possible. I put that cane into the ground. *Why am I hearing that infernal sound?*

Thump, thump.

Then it comes to me. Someone is pounding on the front door.

Four in the afternoon and I look terrible. If I answer the door in my current state it might raise suspicion... but if I play sick...

I throw on my terrycloth robe and head to the door.

Thump, thump, thump!

Whoever is pounding on the door has about as much patience as my dead husband had.

Thump, thump.

It takes me a few minutes to get to the door. I'm still quite tired-- who knew that digging a grave could be so tiring?

The door creaks as I open it.

Charles Langford, my husband's accountant, stands on the front porch and looks a bit nervous.

"Sorry to bother you . . .," he trails off when he sees me. "You okay, Lillian?"

"I'm just a bit under the weather today, Charles."

"Well, I'm sorry you don't feel well and I hate to be a bother, I did try to call first but no one answered." He pauses. "Albert didn't show up for his monthly meeting today. Is he all right?"

"He's fine as far as I know. I've been in bed all day and to be honest, I haven't seen him today." I try to look concerned but feel as if I'm not pulling it off well. "Are you sure he knew about your meeting today?"

"I've been his accountant for more than thirty years. He never missed *one* of our monthly meetings. The man likes to count his money."

This is very true. I have access to the accounts, but the old fuck did keep a tight watch over how much I spent and where. Now that he's "disappeared" I'll have to keep control of my spending. No big ticket items and no major surgery. But I suppose a little injection here and there won't be noticed.

"I'm sorry. We had a bit of a fight last night." I faked a cough. "I just didn't take the time this morning to find out where he was going. But if I see him, I'll tell him you're looking for him."

I start to close the door.

"Are you sure that he's not here, Lillian? I mean his car is in the driveway."

Damn, the fucking car. I didn't think of the car.

Though he could afford it, the bastard never hired a driver, insisting he could just drive himself, or more often than not, I would run his errands for him. But never once did I go with him to his monthly meeting with Charles.

My tired brain works fast, "Oh, he called a car service this morning. I heard him mumble something about that piece of shit not starting again. I think he was going to see about buying a new one. But if he was to see you and he didn't show...."

"Calm down," Charles says. "I'm sure he's fine. He probably just lost track of time." He turns to leave. "If you see Albert, can you ask him to give me a call?"

"Sure, not a problem." I close the door.

Before I could get it all the way closed, Charles asks, "You mind if I look around? I mean..." his face reddens a bit. "I know you're not feeling well, but it would ease my mind to be sure." He looks as if he's going to drop his request for just the briefest of moments and I pause, hoping he will. But he doesn't.

"Sure," I say and open the door wide. I haven't had the chance to look in the study to see if everything is all right, but I am pretty confident that it is.

We walk together. Charles talks as he glances in room after room, but I don't hear him. Instead, I hear it. A faint, *thump, thump*.

It's barely audible, but it's there like a distant bark.

Charles is still talking, but I don't listen. We approach the study and I stop in the doorway. Charles continues in the room. He knows this is the main room my husband resides in and he takes his time to look around.

Thump, thump.

It's louder this time and closer. I look around the room. I did a decent job cleaning up the blood, but sitting where the stain was, is one blue sapphire. One of the vultures's wicked eyes!

No! I must be imagining that. Both sapphires were still in the cane when I tossed it into the grave. I saw them, I *know*!

Thump, thump, thump.

The sound becomes louder. I'm sure Charles can hear it. How can he not?

Thump. Thump. Thump. Thump.

Charles can hear it. I *know* he can. This is all part of the old bastard's plan.

Thump! Thump! Thump!

Louder, louder, louder!

Thump! Thump! THUMP!

How is this possible? I struggle against the urge to go to the back door, throw it open and run out to the garden.

I fake another cough. Maybe Charles will get the hint and leave, but he says something that I don't hear and smiles. Charles is mocking me. He *knows!*

THUMP! THUMP! THUMP!

I'm sweating.

"Are you all right, Lillian?" It's the first words I hear from him since he entered the house.

THUMP! THUMP! THUMP!

I scream. "Can't you hear it?"

A look of concern crosses his face.

THUMP! THUMP! THUMP!

"That!"

He grabs my shoulders.

"Are you all right?" he asks.

I cover my ears.

THUMP! THUMP! THUMP!

I can't take it anymore. "He's in the garden!" I scream as I fall to the floor. "Dig him up! Please, dear God, dig him up! Call someone! Call the police! Please, just make it stop."

Charles kneels beside me. "Make what stop?"

"That sound! That thumping of his goddamed cane!"

✠

Many of A. W. Gifford's story ideas come from the nightmares of his wife, Jennifer. Though she too is a writer of dark fiction, she will never write these stories herself, fearing that if she does, they will come true. He is the editor of Bête Noire Magazine *and his work has appeared in numerous magazines, webzines and anthologies. Though he grew up in the northern suburbs of Detroit, he now resides outside of Atlanta, Georgia with his wife, two dogs, Reagan and Riley, and a pride of cats.*

Loving the Dead

Dorian Dawes

His *desire was to be buried alive…*

When the poet Percy Shelley died, it is rumored that his widow, Mary Wollstonecraft Shelley, of Frankenstein fame, kept his heart in a jar until the day she died. I've often dreamed of a love like that, a love that is everlasting, going far beyond what is sung in pop songs on the radio, or shown in glittery lights in the cinema or on TV—a love that transcends death eternal—sinking into the foul abysmal pit, going where sorrow and fair-weathered affections, even fear of the unholy and the unnatural dare to tread-a love that speaks only in whispers and silence, and is a fire that can burn even in the coldness of buried earth. To have the ability to love long after the putrid stench of death overtakes the body, that is the love which I have come to crave.

This peculiar fascination first caught me in its grip since I was a small child in attendance of a wake at my grandmother's funeral. Her casket was lying open in an adjacent room of the funeral parlor, and amid the veiled faces in black clothes, I recognized my grandfather quietly approaching the fine wooden casket, to gaze mournfully upon her face. I'd already paid my last respects, as final and respectful as an eight year-old can make, and had no wish to see her cold, haggard face again. I found it incredibly eerie to look upon her with all that makeup on her face; her long silver hair brushed and beautiful, cascading gently over her shoulders; as I'd never remembered Grandma ever dressed in such a fashion. I recalled strangely that in life she never wore makeup or frilly dresses, and always insisted on wearing more masculine fashions. All that silliness women put on was just vanity, and she was quite happy rejecting all of it, and what was more,

I remember the life she injected into those brash, declaratory statements. Seeing her body manhandled and shoved into a dress the color of a Pepto-Bismol tablet and makeup slathered all over her face was only another sign that the woman I'd spent many Sunday afternoons with was truly gone, as the real Grandma would have put up a great fuss before they'd ever convince her to wear such silly things.

There were comments from everyone who looked on that lifeless corpse that was but a mockery of the grandmother I knew, which were given with a soft smile and vacant eyes, "She looks so peaceful there."

I felt sickness inside when they spoke, and a chilling coldness that most would assume are uncharacteristic for a child. There was anger that I could not quite articulate into words, an indignance that I was unsure how to properly express, and so I did what any other child my age might, I stormed off to a corner to sulk, and remained thoroughly anti-social, until I saw my grandfather approach her.

Here at last I thought there'd be tenderness, someone who'd look upon the mockery and not give a condescending half-smile and recite some store-bought phrasing to trivialize the death of a loved one, but real emotion and heart-felt loss. Tears, how desperately I wanted there to be tears.

There were none. Instead, he did something thoroughly unexpected, but completely beautiful. While all the funeral guests were conversing and chattering away at the wake like it was some sort of party, my grandfather knelt until his face was inches away from hers, and he kissed her on the lips. I watched from my hiding place in a dark corner of the room behind an artificial fern, peering at him from beneath the plastic leaves, and the germ of fascination grew within me.

Now if you were to ask me how such an innocent and tender moment would have grown into the horrible and depraved imaginations that would possess me later on in my teenage years, I could not tell you. How does innocence transcend into darkest perversion? The slightest thing can tip the mind over the brink into a pit of unimaginable horrors, where even the kindest and gentlest man can give over to his darkest demons. We all have monsters lurking within ourselves, foul imaginings, cruel nightmares and visions that plague us, and we all coat them over with a waxen smile and pleasant greetings, reveling in the lies cast by the noonday sun; always bright, always cheerful, never tearful. Tears are honest things, and anger and violence are the most honest of all, and when we see them, we recoil in distaste and anger, as they call to attention that which we hate most about ourselves, reminding us deep down of the terrible creatures we really are, perhaps giving way to the idea that we are worse for pretending to be otherwise.

At least I am honest about that which causes me greatest shame. I have led a lifelong romance and obsession with the dead, and it has led me to the greatest joys and at often times, the deepest of existential woes. Given what you now know about the peculiarities of my character, it should come as no great shock to you that I have pursued a career in embalming.

Becoming a mortician was no easy task, as the experience during my apprenticeship required an unearthly amount of self-control when I first saw all those bodies, lined up there on tables in my master's cellar. How dearly I wished to caress them, to feel the cold flesh on my skin, the absence of life within their forms, that they might know that there remains someone still whose love for them is *truly* unconditional. Love does not cease when the body goes into the ground, but it continues, no matter what state the person happens to be in, and I love them all.

I grew to dearly enjoy the embalming process, and it is this duty of a mortician which I relish most of all, from the draining of the blood to the care of the body, everything is done with an exacting measure, the tender precision of a caring artist. It is only the final product I loathe, when I look at what I have done to these beautiful bodies, and it is only seeing what has become of them that makes it easy to hand them back over to the greedy clutches of their former loved ones.

Like my grandmother, they scarcely resemble how they did in life, instead becoming a pretty picture of everything that the grieving family wanted them to be. Gone are the flaws which defined their character, the memorable attributes that truly made them unique and beautiful, instead replaced with a grotesque ideal of what it means to be perfect, all in an effort to console the living. Funerals and wakes are not for the dead, but for the living, a silly and meaningless tradition, selfish and self-serving in which the deceased is allowed one final insult before being shoved mercilessly into the ground, or tossed into a fire and imprisoned within a jar so long as their ashes are preserved.

The dead deserve to be loved, and only I know how.

Thus is the root of my dilemma, the agonizing problem which has prompted me to lie awake at night, staring at the ceiling until I drift off into madness, or at best, stark, bleak oblivion, the dreamless sleep, praying never to wake again. Every time I open my eyes to see that yet another day has cursed me, I weep. I am angry with myself, and angry with the world around me that I should be brought into it, that I should be cursed with this nameless passion and be regarded with such hostility for it. I have become all that I hated in my youth, the one who renders the beautiful and the honest nature of decay as false, and for this I suffer. This is my shame, for how can there be any shame in love? My self-hate is borne from my cowardice for not doing all that I want to, for letting those creatures pass from my grip lonely and confused, rendered ugly at my own hands.

How odd is it to me, that we would sanction our dead away, burying them beneath the earth, or imprisoning them in vases for the rest of their existence. What are we so fearful of? If the dead are truly just that, then why would we lock them away, remove them from our sight, mask the supposed ugliness of their rot with a false image of serene beauty? I suppose it goes back to fear, the terror that we will all die at some point, and are fearful to be reminded that this existence to which we cling so fervently is but a temporary state. All the more reason for us to love our departed brothers and sisters, I say, for who but they can teach us the ways of the world beyond, who but the dead can comfort us in these times of terror and grief?

This affliction of the soul is what caused me to plunge further into abhorrent darkness and madness, passions that drove me to actions that yet continue to haunt and torment me. There was once a young man who came to me, seeking to understand the manners of dealing with the dead. It was not an apprenticeship he wanted, but knowledge. I detected in him, however slight, a kind of kinship, for within his eyes there laid a soul with passions so very similar to mine, a kind of coldness that can only come from those who truly appreciate Mother Death in all her sepulchral glory.

For this I trusted him with my secret desires, and because he was beautiful. His hair, thick, curly, and black, had this peculiar way of floating just over his head, with some few locks falling about in a soft, attractive manner over his pale, almost-feminine features; lips that were thin, but had the most delicate curves; and a brow so fine it appeared sculpted. He was exquisite, and when those crystalline-blue eyes locked with mine, I knew, I'd give him whatever he asked.

"Teach me the care of the dead," had been his request, his exact words.

He'd come to me, in that dank cellar of dim flickering fluorescents, in which I practice my craft, to ask me this, and it was only his unearthly beauty that allowed me to forgive this trespass. "And how do you think the dead are cared for?"

I watched his fingers, long and thin and perfect curl around the edge of my embalming table where a fresh corpse lay ready for the blood to be drained and replaced with fluid. The light amid the halls of stone behind him shone around his head like a lurid, green halo and only seemed to add to his remarkable countenance a kind of ghoulish poetry. I watched the flicker of his tongue move snakelike over the edge of those damning lips, so entranced was I by every word that poured from his mouth.

And what a perfect answer it was, "The dead are only loved."

I forgot my duties and we began to discuss at great lengths all the ways in which the dead are meant to be loved. He fascinated and bewitched me with all his fervor and passion for the unknown and the weird, an unbridled sexuality that was loosed through his eyes when he spoke of what it meant to truly love the dead. We became close, and for a short while, he was my sole living companion, and everything was beautiful, but like all things this too was destined for darkness.

It began when the discussion of burials was brought up between us, as the topic of funerals had not yet been covered. I had not a chance to reveal to him my loathing and distaste for the living's treatment of the beautiful dead when he remarked, "I should like to experience it."

A glimmer of hesitation ran through me, though I prodded him into continuing this train of thought.

"Experience what?"

This particular conversation I recall vividly, a foggy day in the graveyard, beneath the lowered eyes of weeping stone angels and cracked crosses, when the clouds hung low and heavy, creating a dense atmosphere of coming doom. A sickness had risen within my stomach as he spoke and for the first time while in his company I prayed for his silence, as so often I'd provoke his thoughts, just to hear him speak.

"To be buried alive," he explained with no small amount of enthusiasm, "Can't you imagine it? Like some old horror story: being mistaken for dead while your family and friends mourn your passing, and then awakening hours later in an oblong box, miles beneath the earth. The exhilaration that must come within those final moments as panic overwhelms you as the horror of your present situation becomes apparent in your mind, the racing of the heart-beat, the gulping of air within your lungs, and you start to pound heavily upon the lid, screaming until you've run out of breath for someone to find you, but they can't! No one can hear you scream, no one can hear the pounding of your fists against the roof of your own coffin. In a fit of desperation you might try to vainly claw your way out of your prison, but you only tear your fingernails to shreds, bloody and useless, covered in splinters.

"I love this so much, because of the bitter irony," his eyes have a luminous quality to them as he speaks; he's spent some time thinking on this, "In the most extreme moments of experiencing death, do you feel the most alive."

I acknowledged his desires awkwardly, quietly, and did my best to change the subject, avoiding the topic of burial for the remainder of the day. From that moment on though our relationship was tainted, as if by giving voice to these deepest desires had brought about an obsession that he was now compelled to dwell upon at all times. Every conversation turned to his morbid fantasies, growing in increasing and more frightful detail.

Soon, it was that I was plagued with endless nightmares of it, waking up miles beneath the earth, in the place I feared even to put the dead, a living claustrophobic hell, so that even the solace of my once-dreamless sleep became a source of unbearable horror. I experienced every second of it through troublesome dreams–the initial shock at finding myself locked within the most dire predicament, feeling my own lungs grow hoarse as I screamed in vain, pounding away at the ceiling of my prison that there has a been a mistake, that I have been buried alive. These dreams and visions had a deteriorating effect upon my health; I grew thinner, and my eyes more wide and sunken, so that soon I resembled the very corpses I worked with; a living cadaver, soulless and empty. I should have been overjoyed at this alteration to my appearance, and had it been for the causes of my mental anguish, I might have, but I'd become so far removed from any semblance of comfort that any pleasure that could be taken from the elegance of a living death was stolen from me.

It would only seem facetious, possibly comical to say that my troubles were yet to increase, and I only wish that it were, that these things were nothing but the punch line of a very terrible joke told in bad taste, possibly told after too many glasses of wine at a party, in which there is awkward laughter and silence, and like that all is forgotten. Life would be easier like that, a trivialization of all of our greatest woes, reduced to merely that, a few bad jokes and some cheesy puns.

Maybe that's why there is always laughter at funerals; life is a joke, death the punch line.

My companion and I had a few drinks late one night, and there was a brief stint of a few hours where I forgot my sorrows and relished his company again, forgetting his troubling obsessions. Fool that I was I could not see the glint in his eye and the peculiar smile upon his curvaceous lips that would have told me that something was not altogether right this evening. I remember asking him some hours before he led me outside into the darkness of the cemetery, what was the cause of all his mirth and celebration. He hadn't answered. I would find out soon enough; he took me by the hand, guiding me beneath a stone archway and into the darkness of the wood, a flickering flashlight to guide our way. He stopped only when we'd reached a cluster of gnarled trees, where the moss hung weeping from their branches, to shine his light upon a hole at least six feet deep, and within that whole an oblong box, and resting against the trees, a shovel.

"I've decided," he said, "It's time."

I have mentioned before that the lure of his eyes and the entirety of his countenance demanded to be obeyed, that no request he uttered of me was too great, that I'd obey him in all things but he were to ask. This proved even now, though I am certain the drink that slowed my mind and tongue prevented any sort of resistance I might have built up, and had I been sober I could have washed my hands of my role in this tragedy: his suicide.

But like a foolish, drunk coward I obeyed him, buried him. I hammered the nails upon his coffin, while there was yet breath in his lungs. I took the shovel and buried him with it, and all the while I wept uncontrollably, my breath heavy with sobs. His smiling gleeful face, like a pretty maniac before I closed the lid upon his handmade coffin, was the last I'd ever see of him.

As I left the scene, covered in dirt and feeling as if I would never be cleansed, I had a horrible imagining, the sound of fists beating against wood. *Bum-bum. Bum-bum.* I knew these were merely my paranoid visions at work, as I'd already returned to the cemetery and his abandoned body was some miles behind me, buried beneath layers and layers of earth, and yet they horrified me. I returned to my home and stared at the darkness of the ceiling for the remainder of the evening, listening steadily to the pounding of imaginary fists against a coffin door. *Bum-bum. Bum-bum.*

Those noises haunted me for the remainder of the evening and for the next week on through. I began to become obsessed with the idea that he'd been able to survive for some time down there, and that the minute the final bit of earth had gone over his tomb, he'd come to his senses, regretting his actions, and began desperately crying out for my attention, crying out for me to save him. I imagined the anguish of those final moments of his existence, of clawing at his tomb, trying to free himself. These thoughts haunted me so much, that I returned to the site of his grave, and began to dig through the earth to find him again. I needed to know that he'd gone in peace, that he had not suffered.

For a brief agonizing moment, my hands quivered upon the lid of his coffin, knowing even before I opened the lid what I would find. I still cried loudly when I saw them, scratch marks embedded heavily upon the inside surface of the wood, his mouth hung open in a permanent wide-eyed wail of terror, regret, and anguish.

Sorrow turned to elation as I realized the thing that I'd been given. Wrapping my arms around his lifeless head, cradling him against my chest, I saw that I now finally had the creature that I could love, finally carrying out my dreams of giving love to the dead, proving that love truly can reach from beyond the grave.

Weep no more beloved, for now you can be loved as no man has ever been loved before. By my side, you shall wait in endless slumber, kept away from the hateful stares of all who view this beautiful thing you and I share as unwholesome, unnatural. We all need our companions. My pretty, my sweet. Dream in darkness with me.

✠

Dorian Dawes *is the Asst. Creative Director, as well as columnist and blogger for the online alternative-culture magazine,* The Catalyst, *and his fiction appears regularly in the literary e-zine* The Corner Club Press. *The lurking terrors and monstrous horrors within his imagination have tormented him since childhood, providing but a brief reprieve once they are exorcized through the written word. His lifetime goal is to use the horrors of his mind to right the horrors of the real-word; the brutal nature of mankind's inhumanity to man.*

Once Upon a Midnight

Scott Overton

In the end, the fate of humanity rested in the hands of a woman scorned.

Lennie Allen wouldn't have characterized herself in that way. But she'd already triggered one warning from the computer's security subroutine by being distracted. The next time she'd be locked out for twenty-four hours. The Director would not be amused.

Normally she welcomed the security protocols; the retina scan, voice recognition, code-words, and fingerprint-scanning mouse were all a part of life in one of the nation's highest-echelon research facilities, and they helped her sleep at night. God knew the stuff they handled could be used with catastrophic effect by the wrong people. It was the *keystroke dynamics* keyboard that turned out to be a pain in the ass. If its biometrics system ever suspected that she was acting under duress it would offer only two warnings and then go into complete lock-down. Mendelssohn swore he'd been locked out once as a result of chugging one too many Starbucks.

Lennie was finding it hard to care about invented global cataclysm when her own world was falling apart.

She loved working in WCSD—the development and analysis of *worst case scenarios* made good use of her vivid imagination and over-flowing cup of personal paranoia. In fact, it was often cathartic. If she could imagine the very worst things that could happen to the planet, and devise potential responses to them, it robbed her own personal fears and troubles of their potency.

But not this time. Ed was gone. Three nights ago. The notification of divorce proceedings had been delivered to her this morning. *God, that was fast. What was his hurry?* Considering that Lennie hadn't suspected a thing until three nights and…twenty-three minutes ago. Maybe that was what hurt the most, that she'd been so blind. Lennie the genius, her friends called her. Not so smart, after all. Wrapped up in her work, imagining the most terrible things that could happen to a world, without realizing that sometimes 'the world' came down to just two people.

She ran her hands over her glossy black work-station. It was her link to the powerful computer nexus that produced the Reichmann Analog Virtual Environment—a long name with a catchy acronym was important to the people who wrote the cheques. Those grey-suited dark-tied backroom government autocrats had seen enough plain old su-percomputers. They needed a name that could jazz up a bland requisi-tion proposal and bamboozle a roomful of auditors. Lennie never used the full title. To her, the RAVE Nexus was part-taskmaster, part-play-ground. From its matrix of graphics imaging software, intelligent problem-solving, and pure brute processing speed sprang forth cre-ations of startling realism. Lennie could step into a three-dimensional projection of a pristine globe, key in the disaster parameters, and watch it bleed in spreading pools around her.

As a biologist her specialty was pandemics. It was a sexy topic—had been since the first years of the century, for some reason. Scientists had latched onto the idea that pandemics followed some kind of regular schedule, and the world was overdue. After that it was a matter of course that every biological outbreak anywhere attracted an inordin-ate amount of attention from a global media fascinated with dying things. And if the scientific community found that modestly fanning the flames meant mounds of research money thrown their way, well, who could really blame them?

Lennie's job was to gather everything, from their most carefully as-sembled data to their wildest flights of fancy, and feed it to the RAVE-n. Then the cyber-mind was charged with assessing the probabilities of every scenario, analyzing the etiology, predicting the spread pat-tern, forecasting the fatality rates, yea, prophesying over the quick and the dead. They ran several scenarios a week. The human race had nearly been eradicated dozens of times.

Lennie and the RAVE-n were very good at their job.

Now, though, disaster had invaded her own reality. She felt it like a poison in her veins. Her vision lost its focus, and her fingers miscar-ried on the keys.

What had gone so wrong in the life they'd shared, she and Ed?

(Eddy. She always called him Eddy because he called her Lennie. He was a sports writer, and everyone in that world was called Bobby or

Jimmy or Scotty, weren't they? He dreamed of being a political reporter. Would he have called the President Barry?)

The screen was angrily flashing an image at her.

It was the corporate logo of the Reichmann Analog Corporation: a representation of the Pallas Athena, goddess of war and wisdom. *Damn*. She entered the "SAFE' code to reset the security function.

She had to concentrate, or the RAVE-*n* would kick her ass. And deservedly so. It wasn't just computer modeling that the RAVE-*n* controlled. All of Level Seven was a full-blown Hazmat lab, operated robotically. The substances studied in there were so dangerous that humans rarely ventured inside, except for the PhD equivalent of janitorial work. The test-tubes and beakers and petri dishes belonged to the RAVE-*n*. Inside were samples of Rickettsiae bacteria, the villain behind typhus and Rocky Mountain spotted fever; Arenaviridae viruses responsible for Lassa fever; Ebola virus; the corona virus that produced SARS; Marburg virus; several different strains of avian type A influenza viruses of the H5, H7, and H9 subtypes capable of infecting humans, and even a few precious grams of the 1918 Spanish Flu, culled from a corpse frozen in the Alaskan permafrost. Some of the most deadly pathogens known to humankind, all held in the capable pincers of a cybernetic brain and its robotic minions. It was the stuff of sci-fi fright movies, but Lennie wasn't worried. The RAVE-*n* had the abilities of an Artificial Intelligence in many ways, but no independent thought. She liked to say that even if the supercomputer *could* take over the world, the RAVE-*n* was too smart to *want* it.

No, there was far more danger from humans screwing up, maybe because they couldn't keep their inconvenient emotions from getting in the way. Lennie reached for a cup of coffee that was hours cold, and put it back down with a grimace.

They were running simulations of avian flu outbreaks again this week. Although it had been years since the first flare-ups of the H5N1 strain in Hong Kong in the late 1990's, and the more frightening outbreaks later in Southeast Asia, the best minds said that H5N1 or something like it was still lurking in the shadows, waiting for its moment to strike. Every so often it would appear in a flock of domestic fowl somewhere around the globe, and a massive slaughter would follow.

There hadn't been a documented case of H5N1 human-to-human transmission beyond one secondary victim. It was a pandemic held in check because the virus couldn't yet spread among the human population. But flu viruses mutate like there's no tomorrow.

A flock of wild ducks might fly over a poultry farm, leaving behind a bombardment of infected droppings. Wandering chickens would spread the virus to the nearby stock of pigs, one or two of which had already been unlucky enough to pick up a dose of *human* flu from the overly attentive Farmer Nguyen. Once inside the accommodating blood stream of the swine, the two visiting viruses could swap a few genes and, presto: a new strain of bird flu capable of spreading among *Homo sapiens*. Within a few days Farmer Nguyen and his family would have ruined lungs, filled with blood, as their bodies' misguided immune systems deployed cellular soldiers that destroyed the very tissues they were meant to save.

In the outside world the process of mutation was random and slow. It was a different story among the gleaming white walls of Level Seven. There a macabre array of stainless steel bones danced within Plexiglas cylinders, slicing and dicing and splicing, finding new recipes of DNA—shiny new double strands of nucleotides mixed and matched from human diseases and those of the animal kingdom, with the deliberate purpose of *creating* new pathogens deadly to humans. The rationale was that, by creating these lethal agents we could learn how to fight them.

Lennie was always grateful that she didn't tend to remember her dreams.

She also felt that her own hands were clean. She didn't create the murderous agents. She only ran simulations of their path of destruction.

When she and the RAVE-*n* turned the new killer loose, it was only on a *virtual* globe—an ethereal construct of numbers and electrical impulses, sanitized and safe. Lennie provided the data and the computer showed her Armageddon.

She would never admit it to anyone, but it was morbidly fascinating to watch the world's dominant species die a thousand gruesome deaths. Particularly if at least one of the virtual victims bore the face of Eddy.

No, that wasn't true. She didn't want him dead. Maybe the blame was hers. She'd always known that secrets could tear a relationship apart. Her father's military career had poisoned her parents' marriage after he'd been promoted into the upper echelons of the Pentagon, and had to hide the details of his workday from his own wife. After that, the trust was gone and the fire along with it—Lennie had watched it happen.

She'd vowed never to make the same mistake, but that was exactly what she'd done. It wasn't just her job's security demands; she'd told herself she was protecting Eddy from the horrors of Level Seven for his own good. It wasn't healthy to live day after day with the threat of a biological holocaust hanging like a Sword of Damocles in the mind's eye. Some people simply couldn't take it, and spent the rest of their lives in therapy.

So she couldn't tell him about her work, and she couldn't tell him why not. But he wasn't a fool. He suspected something. Eventually it turned into the conviction that she was involved in something big...a potential hot story that could be his *entrée* into the political arena. She was sure he hadn't come up with that idea on his own. It had the per-fumed taint of that blonde internet blogger he'd talked about more and more often. The one who was always digging for government conspiracies. The one with the inflated ego and the inflated chest.

God! Was that what had happened? Had an online correspondence sparked an offline romance? Oh Eddy...Eddy...did I drive you to that? She felt a hot tear well up, and had to snap her head away before it could splash onto the keyboard.

She didn't want him dead. She was furious, cruelly hurt, and hope-lessly infatuated all at the same time. She loved him beyond reason, and even now she knew that she would take him back without hesita-tion, if he asked. But what were the odds of that? Predicting them would take more skill than she had. It would require a master of pre-dictions.

No. No, the idea was ridiculous. She turned her head away from the screens and imprisoned her hands beneath her legs to restrain them, while she rocked back and forth in confusion.

There was no-one else in the lab. There likely wouldn't be for anoth-er forty-five minutes—her coworkers liked to take long lunches. And she knew how to erase almost all traces of her commands, except in the RAVE-*n*'s deepest core memory.

Did she dare?

Inevitable as a pandemic itself, she surrendered seven minutes later and began to key in the data. The RAVE-*n* already had reams of in-formation about Lennie. She quickly fed it a rough profile of Eddy, warts and all, resisting the powerful temptation to embellish the warts.

Query: *Will Lennie and Eddy get back together?*

There was no sign of activity from the RAVE-*n*—there never was. But sixty seconds was an eternity of processing time for a task that in-volved no global modeling, no quantum variables, and no fancy graphics in 128-bit studio-precision color.

The screen finally came to life.

RAVE-*n*: *Insufficient data.*

She exhaled a long-held breath and realized that her hands were trembling. She didn't dare try it again. It was sheer idiocy to have done it in the first place. She spent the next five minutes covering her tracks.

The rest of the afternoon was excruciating. Each time someone came over to speak to her, she expected them to hiss a withering accusation about using lab facilities for a personal whim. She vowed that she would never give in to such an unworthy impulse again. She hurried home that night in relief, and dreamed of a spinning globe projected in mid-air, with her face on one side and Eddy's on the other, and she could only watch helplessly as scenario after scenario brought spreading patches of emptiness like a cancer between them.

At the first coffee break the next morning, she asked again.

RAVE-*n*: *Insufficient data.*

This time she didn't delete the query, she merely hid it behind layers of other tasks. But it waited there for her to call it up, first at lunch, then at afternoon break, and eventually whenever she had the room to herself. In between, her mind would wander from cross-indexing fatality rates to trying to recall any memories of her marriage that might help in her cupidean quest.

RAVE-*n*: *Insufficient data.*

In frustration she nearly pounded a fist on the keyboard, but that might trigger another computation. Because of the dynamic interface, the machine already finished most of her sentences for her — they'd worked together for so long it anticipated nearly every keystroke. Instead she chastised herself again for obsessing over a husband — EX – husband — and tried to force her tense fingers to relax on the keys.

She was startled to see the screen begin to fill with words...words beginning with EX.

Exacerbate
Exact
Exacting
Exaggerate

She quickly keyed in a 'Terminate' command. The RAVE-*n* was getting too damned helpful for their own good.

But not helpful where it really counted. Why couldn't the supercomputer produce an answer for *her*? Why didn't it even try?

The question was too simple — that must be it. She needed to approach it like any other scenario. Build a model, enter the data, run the simulation. But that would take time. She could never accomplish that much in a couple of coffee breaks. She had to....

She had to work overtime. Which meant she needed a cover story. Say her last pandemic simulation had run into bugs—of the computer, not biological variety—but she was close to tracking them down and didn't want to lose the momentum?

Her supervisor accepted the fiction readily enough. Lennie was one of his best workers. And anyway she was on a salary.

She had to be careful. There was still a possibility that someone else might be working late and walk in on her. It was even possible that one of the security people would make a random check on her work station. She needed a shadow screen—a secondary display she could bring up with a stroke of a key. Only a real task would be convincing enough to fool a colleague, but she'd just finished the last of her most recent series of simulations. What else would look plausible?

She called up the RAVE-*n*'s latest results from Level Seven. And instantly regretted it. A quick scan of the data caused the blood to drain from her face.

Good God. This was the worst one yet: a strain of virus that appeared to be based on a hemagglutinin 5 and neuraminidase 1, but had stitched-on RNA from half a dozen sources. The testing just completed that afternoon showed a startling 100% lethality—virtually unheard of. Early indications revealed a six or seven-day incubation period, followed by fatality within four days. That alone made it much more dangerous than killers like Ebola—they killed their hosts so quickly that they rarely spread very far from the original source of the infection. This new creation had no such weakness. It was the perfect traveler. *God help us if....*

She didn't let her mind complete the thought. Instead she began the practiced routine of building the computer model that would complete it for her. The horrific allure of the new pathogen was nearly enough to distract Lennie from her original purpose.

It was the moment when the world could have been saved.

But destiny or fate or evolution dictated otherwise. The pull of her aching heart was stronger. Once the basic parameters of her scenario had been established, she allowed the RAVE-*n* to fill in the rest, adding only the simple command to Run the program and then Terminate. Then she turned back to her private project. The reunion of Lennie and Eddy. The *best* case scenario.

✠

It happened only minutes before midnight. She awakened to the sound of the alarms, and the pain where the keys had become embedded in her cheek.

Had they caught her?

The klaxon reverberated through the room, piercing her ears until her jaw ached. Warning lamps painted the walls in spasms of colour. Finally gathering her wits together she snapped her head up to look at what they called "The Big Screen", a liquid crystal panel mounted from the ceiling that displayed announcements for all staff, and alerts of any kind. It was mutely screaming in giant fluorescent letters.

There was a breach on Level Seven. A deadly toxin was loose.

Already an army of biohazard experts would be scrambling into hazmat suits—she could picture them racing down echoing hallways to bring the enemy to battle. Yet, even as she watched, her initial alarm turned to helpless horror.

The vents were opening!

The outside vents of the lab were intended to exhaust toxic gases in the event of a fire. They were a dangerous necessity, but there were countless failsafe systems to prevent them ever opening in the aftermath of a spill—exactly the kind of accident she was now witnessing. The fail-safes could not be overridden manually by a murderous saboteur or terrorist maniac. That had been demonstrated again and again, before the lab could even be built. No-one could open the vents to the open air once a breach alert had been sounded.

No human.

The RAVE-*n*! The computer must have allowed it. *Good God, could it have been caused by something* she'd *done?*

Her fingers flew frantically over the keyboard, recalling the recent list of commands and actions, luminous letters reflected in her wet eyes.

No! It wasn't possible!

The last command line accused her from the screen like an executioner's pointing finger:

"Run program. EX-Terminate."

She slumped back in the chair, and her vacant eyes came to focus on the holographic globe suspended in mid-air before her, running its final simulation.

Blotches of invading crimson ate their way around the ghostly blue projection of her home world, almost more quickly than she could see. In a daze, she tapped a trio of keys to check the time scale and drew a ragged breath, then expanded the range to slow the simulation down. This time she could see the wash of salmon colour, representing the transmission of the virus, racing around the globe in a flash. Immediately afterward followed the blood red flood of fatality, moving slowly for the first ten or fifteen seconds, then almost instantly transforming the whole mottled Earth into a pulsing red beacon of warning. Stunned, she stood and walked into the center of the projection, then turned slowly in place, and swept her gaze over each quadrant. There was nowhere left untouched, no safe haven of shelter or resilience. Not even in the Himalayas, or the desert of the Sudan, or the barren Antarctic.

A flicker of movement drew her attention back to the Big Screen overhead. Its glaring fluorescent letters had been replaced with an epitaph of damning words.

Query: *Will Lennie and Eddy get back together?*

RAVE-*n*: *Nevermore.*

✠

Scott Overton *is a former radio morning man in Ontario, Canada, now choosing to craft written words instead and sleep later than 4:00am. His short fiction has been published in* On Spec, Neo-opsis, *and the anthologies* Doomology: the Dawning of Disasters *and* Canadian Tales of the Fantastic. *His SF novels are now looking for good homes in the publishing industry. When not writing, Scott's passions include scuba diving and a couple of collector cars, in which he hopes to someday find enough story inspiration to make them tax deductible. Scott's webpage is: www.scottoverton.ca.*

The Amazing Valdemar

Linda Donahue

Tonight marked the four hundred and fifty-ninth performance of the Amazing Valdemar that I'd attended. For over two years, I'd followed the mesmerist across country and overseas, catching the early and late shows on Friday and Saturday nights. I'd sat in the balconies of historic theatres in Paris and London, and in dives seedier than this Las Vegas nightclub.

Since my wife's death, I'd pursued nothing else.

And in about six months, I expected to be penniless. I'd liquidated everything, except for one suitcase jammed with clothing, in order to bring my wife's killer to justice.

On stage, the Amazing Valdemar passed his hand before the face of an unsuspecting participant recruited from the audience. An athletic man, younger than my forty years, swayed on his feet, his eyes closed. I knew then his mind was completely under the mesmerist's command.

This man fit the preferred victim profile I'd constructed. Thirty-something, healthy, athletic and a tourist or traveler. The man still wore a sticky-backed name-tag reading COLLYER. My wife and I had been vacationing in Venice when she'd climbed onto Valdemar's stage. For a moment, the seedy dive seemed to be the small nightclub tucked between restaurants, overlooking the canal.

From a shadowy corner in back I tensed, my heart a dull, aching thud in my chest. I watched Valdemar closely, straining to hear every syllable he spoke.

Valdemar strode through clouds of cigarette smoke, addressing the audience in a smooth, Danish accent. "He has fallen under a deep hypnotic spell. In such a state, his mind is open to the most astounding possibilities. With a simple inquiry, our subject can locate memories long forgotten, a simple trick any hypnotist can perform. But even more amazing, with the proper suggestion, his mind can reach outward, into the universe's collective consciousness to retrieve languages long dead. Fantastic, you say? In my studies of the arcane and occult, I have uncovered the incredible. The brain is a phenomenal organ" — he spread his arms and smiled — "when properly commanded by a master." Valdemar circled the man, his gloved hand sweeping near the man's face, but not quite touching it. "The brain controls our bodies, awake or asleep. Its bounds are limitless and beyond comprehension."

Valdemar was an unassuming man, slight of build. Though he appeared to be in his fifties, the gleam in his eyes spoke of wisdom gathered over many lifetimes. Stars and moons covered his blue wizard robes. He wore a turban with an egg-sized crystal and purple ostrich plumes. Silver gloves covered his long, thin fingers. Though he dressed like a sideshow charlatan, he possessed true magical abilities.

But his practice was of the darkest, vilest arts.

The drunken audience only half paid attention. A few shouted absurd requests: "Make him walk like a chicken," or "Make him bark like a dog." A more original, self-serving man hollered, "Make him give me a hundred bucks!"

Valdemar never took suggestions from the crowd. He always had his own agenda. For Collyer, the man on stage, I feared Valdemar's intent was death. And I knew nothing could stop Collyer's impending demise. If shouting could wake him from his deadly stupor, the audience's calls would've done so. Likewise, no one ever heeded my warning not to go on stage. If Valdemar recognized me, noticed me sitting nightly among the audience, he didn't fear me. He never flinched when his dark gaze met mine.

A drunken woman waved a feathered boa, shouting, "Tell him to wear this and pretend he's a showgirl!"

For such an unsophisticated audience, I doubted Valdemar would have Collyer summon up Cesar's words. In that respect, the crowd had some small effect on Valdemar's performance.

Standing before the swaying, mesmerized man, Valdemar said, his eyes glittering, "Do a handstand."

That brought appreciative hoots from the crowd. Had they possessed much in the way of cash, they would, no doubt, tip the mesmerist well — though the volunteer was who entertained them.

With his eyes closed, Collyer placed his palms on the dirty wooden stage then kicked up his heels. He stood on his hands with greater balance than when on his feet. Loose change, a hotel key card and a couple of casino chips tumbled from his trousers and jacket pockets.

The audience applauded while one drunk hollered, "Make him walk on his hands!"

Yet Valdemar ended the volunteer's unknown embarrassment, ordering him to stand on his feet. With a command and loud clap, Valdemar released Collyer from his stupor.

"Tell us, *Robert*, are you enjoying your visit to Las Vegas?" Valdemar asked, his voice robust, easily reaching the back tables where I sat.

The more sober and attentive audience members oohed. Collyer hadn't stated his first name and neither was it on his name-tag. In over two years, I'd never seen Valdemar *guess* wrong. Once he had his victim under control, he simply knew things, mostly likely via some *cosmic* source.

Collyer squinted, glanced at his name-tag and frowned. "How did you know my name's Robert?"

Valdemar smiled rather disarmingly and spread his silver-gloved hands. "The same way I know you sell car insurance and are in town for a convention. I know, because I am the Amazing Valdemar!" He spun and made a grand flourish with his hands. Then he gazed upward and said, "My cosmic sources tell me your luck has turned for the better—but caution you not to be greedy, or you'll lose more than you can afford."

My gut squirmed. In the pit of my stomach, I knew Robert Collyer had already lost far more than he could afford. Not that he would realize it until the first symptoms appeared. And like those before him, his death would remain an unsolved mystery.

After the performance, I was so certain that Collyer would be next to succumb to Valdemar's black magic that I forwent the late-night show to follow the unsuspecting victim. He hailed a cab. Fortune smiled on *me*, at least; a second cab pulled up instantly.

As if caught up in a black-and-white detective movie, I instructed my driver to "follow that cab".

Collyer's cab pulled up in front of the Luxor Hotel, its pyramid shape rising amid neon lights. For a moment I stared at the replicated sphinx, remembering Egypt's golden sand, one of many exotic places I'd followed Valdemar. Tonight I followed my new quarry to a roulette table.

Casually, I approached Collyer. "Say, weren't you on stage tonight at the show?"

"Vegas is crawling with shows," Collyer said, his tone unfriendly and disinterested. And his eyes lacked life's luster. They were the eyes of a dead man who didn't know he'd already died.

My gaze flicked away involuntarily, unable to bear the pain of staring death in the face again. "I'm sure it was you at the Amazing Valdemar. Robert Collyer, right?" I hoped to appear genuine, for I had bad news, the sort easier to share once we'd formed a connection. Thrusting out my hand, I said, "I'm Andreas Kerner. Though Valdemar gets all the credit, *you* were amazing."

"No offense, Mr. Kerner, but you can't sell to a salesmen."

"If you don't mind, I'd love to see if the Amazing Valdemar's predictions come true. To see if your luck has truly changed, I mean."

"What else would you mean?" he asked.

Just then, the roulette dealer announced, "Number thirty-two! A winner."

I felt a twinge of sadness for the grinning man who scooped up his chips. When asked if he wanted to place another bet, Collyer headed towards the blackjack tables.

"Are you following me?" Collyer snapped.

"Only out of pure academic interest, I assure you."

Collyer sat at a table run by a pretty young blonde. When he lost the first hand, I wondered if I'd guessed wrong... if Collyer might be lucky after all. If so, it could mean Valdemar's true mark was just now taking a table to watch the second show.

Yet as next couple of hands played out, Collyer won big.

"Amazing," I said, trying to hide my sorrow.

"People *do win* sometimes. It's not that unbelievable." Nonetheless Collyer finally thrust out his hand. "What did you say your name was?"

"Andreas Kerner."

"Well, Andreas, let me buy you a drink. How about we celebrate my lucky streak?"

I agreed, because Collyer would need a drink when I told him the news. We sat in the bar. He downed three martinis to the one neat scotch that I nursed.

"You know," I said, "I first saw the Amazing Valdemar in Venice. Like you, my wife volunteered to be mesmerized."

"She here tonight too? Or did you come to Vegas alone?"

I sipped my drink. Staring in the golden depths, the cord lights shining through the liquid, "She's dead."

"I'm sorry. If it were up to me, I'd trade places with you."

I tried not to glare, though in that moment I didn't pity him his fate. Perhaps he thought he was being funny, or perhaps it was the booze talking. Or maybe, subconsciously he knew what had happened.

"So," Collyer drawled, "you were at the show. What did I do? Did the Amazing Valdemar make me quack like a duck?"

"You did a handstand."

"Apparently my gym membership is paying off." Collyer punched my arm as if we were long-time buddies.

"Robert, I mean this as a friend, see a doctor. Have him check you out. Tell him to test for anything and everything. Tell him that"—I paused for another fortifying sip—"you're dying."

Collyer spat vodka into his glass. "Tell him what? Is that your spiel? Some morbid sales pitch? What exactly is your line of business?"

"I—" My mouth hung a moment. I hadn't done anything since Leslie's death. I could barely remember my life before. She was my wife when she should have been my everything. In losing her, I realized how much I'd lost. But a distant memory bubbled to the top. "I used to teach literature at Stanford."

I was a learned man, versed in Olde English, Chaucerian and Middle English. After graduating from Cambridge, I'd met Leslie in London. It was love at first sight.

My scotch looked blurry, as did my surroundings. I wiped away tears I'd thought I could no longer cry. The bartender, a man who looked like a Chippendale dancer, offered me an extra napkin.

"Didn't mean to dredge up bad memories," Collyer said. "But you got some nerve telling a guy you just met he's gonna die—like you're some Amazing Valdemar yourself."

"There's nothing amazing about me." I wrote my cell phone number on a napkin and shoved it toward him. "When your time comes and you have questions, give me a call. No matter what you think of me, see a doctor. Maybe he can save you."

Maybe. Though doubtful. Yet I couldn't say with any degree of absoluteness. All I knew for certain was when Collyer died, he would be another mysterious case of SOPS—Sudden Organ Purification Syndrome. Cases sprang up across the world without apparent cause. Research had determined only that neither toxins, bacteria nor viruses were to blame. Yet these deaths were spectacular enough that tracking victims on the internet and news was simple.

I knew the cause—Valdemar—but not the means or reason. And had no concrete evidence, at least not the sort the police could act upon. I only knew that on Valdemar's travels, he selected victims, never two in the same city. As long as eight weeks passed between "isolated outbreaks of SOPS." As near as I had determined, only after one victim died did Valdemar select another.

"See a doctor. What harm can it do?" I pressed. "You just won a pile of money. Isn't it worth it to be sure I'm not a crackpot?"

"Listen, maybe my blood pressure's a little high and so's my cholesterol, but otherwise, I'm fit as a fiddle."

"That's the first symptom."

✠

I followed Valdemar's tour to San Francisco.

A month passed and still Robert Collyer hadn't called. Neither did I find reports of a new outbreak of SOPS on the internet. Nor did I see anything in newspaper headlines.

My phone rang, but I didn't recognize the number. Of course, my changed lifestyle had cost me more than my house, car and bank account. I'd lost all my friends as well. If it wasn't a wrong number or a telemarketer, it had to be. . . .

"Mr. Collyer?" I answered.

"How'd you know?" He wheezed as though his lungs were filled with fluid. "The docs say they can't help me, that I've got SOPS. They give me about ten days. For Christ's sake, Andreas, they say my insides are rotting, turning to liquid!"

His outburst brought on a series of ragged, bubbling coughs. I closed my eyes and pulled the phone away from my ear, trying not to remember Leslie's last days. From the sound of his rattling cough, I estimated he had two or three days left.

"It's a horrible end," I said, my heart wrenching. I remembered holding Leslie's hand. How tired she looked, how lifeless her eyes. "My wife died three weeks after—" I swallowed hard.

"You said if I had questions . . . why is this happening to me? What do you know about SOPS?"

I had no idea why I'd given him my number or what made me say I had answers. A moment of weakness, I can only assume. If only I'd learned anything new, could say sometime more comforting than he was the victim of a black magic sorcerer. No one believed in such nonsense, not even in the face of the otherwise inexplicable SOPS.

I still didn't know what drove Valdemar to commit such atrocious acts. Perhaps therein lay the answer; it was some devil's price he'd negotiated for his mystic powers.

If so, Valdemar was no man but a demon who deserved no better than the death he dealt to others.

"Mr. Collyer… Robert," I said at last with some resolve, "I don't have an answer yet, but I will tonight. I won't let another evening pass without knowing."

"How will you learn in one night what no other researcher has figured out? What are you talking about?"

During the pause, in which Collyer wheezed and gasped for breath, I considering hanging up.

But Collyer spoke, his voice hopeful. "You think there's a cure?"

"If there is, I'll do whatever it takes to get it. You have my word."

"Andreas, about that crack I made about your wife — about changing places with you — I was wrong. These last days, the only thing I've regretted is… you know. I'll be waiting for your call. I hope you can help."

"So do I, Robert."

I sat on a bench overlooking the bay. Pigeons cooed at my feet while circling seagulls made a raucous noise. A ship's horn moaned across the bay. Having made a dying man an empty promise, the sounds of life surrounding me were empty of joy.

Did I think Valdemar would confess if I confronted him? No doubt he'd laugh. When I first told the police that he'd killed my Leslie, they very nearly laughed. That I was a grieving man was all that kept their tone polite and serious.

In my heart I knew I was going to kill the Amazing Valdemar. Knowing Robert Collyer, hearing his hope that I could deliver him from death, had given me the strength to do what I should've done two years ago. Who could say how long Valdemar had been killing before murdering my sweet Leslie?

Tonight it ended.

I didn't care if I went to prison. Life without Leslie was worse than any jail sentence.

I arrived early at the old art-house theater in a shady part of town and hung around the alley entrance. I'd never seen the Amazing Valdemar enter or leave, so I assumed he slipped in the back, like the scoundrel he was.

Around sunset, a car pulled up at the end of the alley. I hid in shadows, watching as Valdemar stepped out. His vivid robes swirled at his skinny ankles. Though the coastal air was muggy, he wore a cloak with the oversized hood pulled up. He clutched the cloak's edges, wearing the ever-present, silver gloves.

The car pulled around front while Valdemar slipped inside. I slipped in behind him.

I trailed him to his dressing chamber and shut the door behind me. I started to lock it, but the latch was broken. No matter. I didn't intend to stay long.

"I believe, Mr. Valdemar, that you won't be going on stage this evening." In my head, the threat had sounder tougher and classier. Nonetheless, I stood my ground, clutching the dagger I'd purchased this morning. Before I killed him, however cliché and trite it would be, I wanted to force a confession. It was a literary device I'd often lectured was unrealistic. Now, I understood the need for answers and closure.

Valdemar pulled back his hood and stared at me with a mirthless gaze. I hadn't realized how papery his skin was or that veins showed plainly across his face. Nor had I known he was bald. His head was skull-like, appropriate for a merchant of death.

"I mean it," I said, affecting a menacing tone as I brandished my dagger. "There'll be no performance tonight."

"I see in your eyes that you're right," Valdemar said, ignoring my blade.

"Before I've avenged those you've murdered, tell me why you do it. And how." Until this moment, when I sensed the answer hovering on the air before me, I hadn't realized how much not knowing had eaten at me like a slow cancer. I craved the answer more than revenge.

"Sit," Valdemar offered. "We are civilized and learned men in a world of ignorant apes."

I clenched the dagger's hilt. It was all I could do to stop myself from thrusting it into Valdemar's narrow chest. Shaking, sweat dripping down the back of my neck; I said harshly, "I prefer to stand. And my wife was not an ignorant ape. Yet you murdered her."

"If I did, you have my humblest apologies. I only do what I must to survive. I, too, am a victim in this."

"Then you admit to killing people with hypnotism."

"Yes. My powers *cause* the death of certain people. Not all people. And only when necessary."

"When is it *necessary*? Why do you do it?"

Valdemar laughed. The sound wasn't hearty or hale, but like that of a terminally ill man. "When necessary to live, of course. I was once mortal. I lived a good life. When I grew ill in December of 1845, I died. However, before death claimed me and after my physicians, Dr. Draper and Dr. Francis, determined my death imminent, I summoned my hypnotist, who had on many an occasion helped me to sleep. He had broached me regarding an experiment he wished to perform, in which he would place me in a hypnotic state, arresting my death temporarily. He believed I would feel nothing, that peace would replace my suffering. Yet peace never came, nor did my suffering end."

"That's impossible."

"Yet you claim my act brings about the demise of others? I find that ironic."

Having no rational argument, I waved at him to continue.

"For months I lay on my deathbed, dead, yet in stasis, able only to communicate while unable to move, a prisoner trapped within my own body, feeling my insides turn putrescent. During that time, I formed a bond with the cosmos, a link that has only grown stronger over time. It told me that tonight you would step from the shadows to seek the truth." He picked at his gloves, pulling on each finger to loosen them. "For months I lay at the mercy of my captors. Until some humanity within my hypnotist's heart at last urged him to release me. From the horror on his face, even he did not foresee the repercussions."

"You awoke a monster," I said, at last having a piece of the answer, however preposterous it seemed.

"My awakening produced a profound unrest within the very hearts of my physicians and hypnotist. Perhaps from guilt, for the part he played, Dr. Draper falsified medical records, the contents of which fell into the hands of the master penman Mr. Poe."

I'd thought Valdemar's name sounded vaguely familiar, but my expertise and preferences ran toward classical British authors and not the stylized rambling of writers who peddled their tales in pedantic, Early American journals. In the future, I'd read Poe's works with a much more open mind and a greater appreciation.

"Upon awakening," Valdemar continued, "I instinctively mesmerized the nurse who'd cared for my lifeless body. The act linked our minds, giving me the most keen insight. I knew things I couldn't possibly know about her. Though I'd severed the hypnotic contact almost immediately, the link had already drained her of life, of all but that final drop that sustained her over the following weeks. Over the many reflective years, I've come to think that by devouring a person's life experiences, I exhausted that person's life. Returning to my initial foray, gathering immortality, while the nurse's insides turned to mush, my own, which had sloshed most disgustingly, grew firmer."

Valdemar sat on the stool before the make-up mirror and twisted the loosened gloves in what appeared an honest, sorrowful gesture. Even his ghoulish expression pulled downward in a deep, remorseful frown.

"I was alive again by some miracle," Valdemar said. "Yet I was ghastly, even more desiccated than now." He removed his gloves, revealing hands and fingers that were skeletal thin. "Having lain sick so long, an insatiable hunger grew, telling me I could live off the lives of others. That I never need fear death. If it helps any, I try not to over-feed. I could feast and have the health of a twenty-year old. Instead, as a self-inflicted punishment, I choose to suffer immortality in this frail body."

"Even the immortal Bard died. So will you."

Valdemar smiled. "Perhaps. But not tonight."

Strong hands grabbed me, pinning my arms to my side. The hands squeezed so hard, my fingers went numb. The dagger clattered to the floor. I hadn't heard the door open, hadn't heard Valdemar's assistant enter. Fleetingly, the irony struck; had I killed Valdemar outright, rather than forced a confession—the undoing of many literary heroes —I would have survived victorious.

Instead, Valdemar gripped my chin, his bony hand amazingly strong. He looked past me, saying, "After I feed, tell the manager I won't be performing tonight. Tell him I'm ill. Tell him I'm cancelling all my appearances here." To me he smiled, adding, "You see. You were prophetic."

He passed his other hand before my face. In vain, I attempted to look away but couldn't. His pulsing, blood-red eyes captured my gaze. That hellish gaze bored into my mind. Mental tentacles wove through my brain, digging deeper, spreading and taking hold like poisonous roots. Writhing grave worms worked their way toward my organs, sapping me of life.

Before my dazed eyes, I saw vigor filling Valdemar's breast. His wrinkled flesh thickened and took on color. And the vague hint of thinning white hair crested his brow.

My own death, at least, would be quick. Quick would be merciful and relative. The better part of me had died with Leslie.

Linda Donahue, *an Air Force brat, spent her childhood traveling. Having a pilot's certification and a SCUBA certification, she has been a threat by land, air or sea. For 18 years she taught computer science and mathematics. Currently, she teaches tai chi and belly dance. Linda's stories appear in numerous anthologies, including* Sword & Sorceress 23 *and* Esther Freisner's Strip Mauled *and* Fangs for the Mammaries. *She has two novels,* Jaguar Moon *and* Apocalypse Now! *with a third* Redheads in Love *due in 2012. Linda and her husband keep a rabbit, sugar gliders and cats.*
www.LindaLDonahue.com

Read First

Davin Creed

The events that I am going to explain in this letter are, to the best of my ability, what actually happened. Provided are all the tapes, records and the videos that I could get my hands on, which should corroborate my telling of the events. I understand that some of what I may present will be no more than subjective; however I feel that without my testimony explaining both the objective facts along with my subjective feelings, much meaning would be lost. Beyond all, I wish to explain that even though the events may seem exaggerated or even fabricated, that I am being as objective as humanly possible. Even when I explain what I felt and what I cannot provide evidence for, I do so without making any conclusions, I'm just stating what happened and leave the conclusions to those who would dare to study further.

Several years ago when I still had a respectable reputation, a young boy was referred to me in order to prescribe him some medication. With so many countless referrals in my normal week, most patients come and go without so much as a lingering thought to attest to their existence. However this one boy would not only last in my memory, but would also haunt my every thought until my passing. Yes, several years ago on an unremarkable day, this boy peaked my interest. Our first session was very routine by almost all accounts. The following is a transcription of a portion of the recording of that very first session:

P: "Hello M___, how are you today?"

M: "I'm fine... how are you?"

P: "Good, do you know why you're

here?"

M: "Because I can't sleep?"

P: "That is correct. Can you tell me why you're having trouble sleeping?

M: "I don't want to."

P: "You don't want to tell me or you don't want to sleep?"

M: "I don't want to sleep."

P: "Can you tell me what you normally dream about?"

M: "Lots of stuff, mostly daemons."

P: "Does any of this frighten you?"

M: "Not too much anymore, I'm used to it now. But I don't like it."

It was how the boy answered the questions along with the answers themselves that garnered my interest. He was calm and his answers were clear while not appearing to be practiced. This alone would not have brought this boy from the void of lost memories where most of the people I meet remain, however the tests I conducted and his answers to my questions elevated him into a persistent place in my thoughts. The boy had PTSD (Post Traumatic Stress Disorder for those unfamiliar with the acronym) even though nothing in his chart indicated any event that would normally trigger the disorder. Save for the night terrors, the boy had lived a normal sheltered life. While I am familiar with hypnosis and had practiced in it, it wasn't common that I would employ the technique. I recorded the hypnosis session as well so that I could be sure that the answers I got were not encouraged by me, as well as to allow colleagues to review and scrutinize it. The boy had a night terror the prior night, which was a welcome coincidence that might have helped his recollection with it being so fresh in his memory.

P: "I'm going to ask you about things that happened last night, just answer as clearly as you can, with as much detail as you can remember."

M: "Okay."

P: "What did you eat for dinner?"

M: "We had hamburgers... well ah... cheeseburgers."

P: "What were you doing right before going to bed?"

M: "I was playing some games."

P: "Now skip ahead to when you're in bed; tell me what happens."

M: "I'm just laying there with my eyes closed. Then I hear them."

P: "Hear who?"

M: "The voices, the darkness."

P: "What are the voices saying?"

M: "I don't know, too many of them, too quiet. Some of them screaming."

P: "What are they screaming?"

M: "Nothing, just screaming like they're mad. Aaggggh! They're coming closer!"

P: "You're safe here, nothing can hurt you, you're just an observ..."

M: "No, THEY'RE EVERYWHERE! HELP ME! SOMEONE! HELP..."

P: "What happened, did you wake up?"

M: "I haven't been asleep yet."

To the inexperienced ear, this hypnosis session may seem on the extraordinary side, but let me assure you that with the proper (or more accurately with an improper hypnotist), something even more grand could be encouraged out of virtually any subject. So while most not in the field may find the session disturbing or incredulous, I must assure you that I provided it in my account because it helps me detail what happened accurately and not because of any notion of theatrical and/or emotional influence. All I could be sure of at this point was that the boy had very disturbing experiences. I had concluded at the time, as any rational person should have, that those experiences were only in his mind. My own curiosity and my desire of writing a research paper on unusual triggers of PTSD based off of this boy, led me to request further sessions with the him. We discussed the things the boy dreamed about and what he thought he saw for several weeks before I suggested that we perform an overnight sleep observation. During the sleep session we would use cameras, microphones and various body function monitors so that we could monitor everything from respiration to brain activity while he slept.

He came in for one sleep observation every two weeks, which was more than enough for my studies. The first several observations, while not normal, were nothing unexpected after having discussed several times the types of dreams the boy had. He spent most of the nights lying still with his eyes closed but rarely falling asleep, let alone how little he entered REM sleep. While these nights provided a great amount of data for my research and what I thought would lead to my treatment for the boy, they were nothing compared to the night that changed my view of the boy's condition and my view of the world.

Everything from the time the boy arrived that night to when he was left alone in the room was just like all the other nights of almost no activity. It seemed however that this night the boy began to have trouble early on from his much more than normal tossing and turning and not closing his eyes. He eventually settled down and appeared to have finally gotten to a restful state ready for sleep. Almost an hour had passed after the boy had been lying still with his eyes closed, when he suddenly opened his eyes wide. This is on the video provided on the disk, as no one was there observing him at the time. A few moments later, after I heard the screaming, is when I came in to see what was going on. And while both the instruments and my ears could hear the screaming, the boy laid there perfectly still. His eyes were open and without so much as a quivering on his closed lips, the screaming could not have been coming from him. Yet the screaming continued in spite of having no discernible source.

At this point I was more curious than concerned, I wanted to find the source of the screaming. The boy, while appearing to be frightened, was in no danger. Then something moved in the room, almost imperceptible. I barely noticed the movement on the monitor from the corner of my eye. When I looked where I saw the movement on the screen there was nothing. It happened once more and then once again, however every time I focused on the movement: I could see nothing. The screaming quieted into murmuring voices when I could finally see what was moving in the room: the shadows were slowly engulfing the room, even where light was being cast directly onto the surfaces. The voices, too many to count, began to grow louder while not enhancing my ability to make out what any of them were saying. Were it not for the video records, I would have thought it was merely my imagination that made the shadows appear to be crawling toward the boy from all directions. But even in the video one can distinctly make out hands and heads inching closer to consume the very frightened boy. I stood there staring as a deer into headlights for the fear had entrenched my legs from the horror I was witnessing and the disbelief that it was happening.

At the sight of this I did what I never would have conceived of doing given the circumstances in speculation or had spent some time thinking about it: I went into the room to retrieve the boy. The door struggled against my push, but after some fighting, I was able to open it enough for me to enter. On the floor my foot rested not on the tiles that I expected but a moving surface that gave in a little under my weight and produced the most wretched moan from below. What returned with the groan was a cold sharp slash across my calf that most reluctantly produced tears of blood from the fresh scrapes. The blood drops took their course down my calf to be caught in my sock as I made my way towards the bed. My legs, chest and back were treated to more of the same abuse as the voices continued to get louder. When I was close enough to touch the boy he was almost completely covered in this mix of darkness and daemonic figures. As I tried to pull the boy out of the bed, the shadows seemed to give me a considerable fight. Picking the boy up released what little protection I had against the abuse I had been receiving and increased in intensity so much that I had been knocked down several times on my way back to the door.

The door was even more difficult to open than when I had entered, I used every available part of my body and every bit of strength I had left to open it and place my legs to prevent its closure. I carried the boy over me and out the door before finally struggling the rest of my body through. The door closed so forcefully that I almost lost my fingers. I sat there looking at the boy who seemed frozen not realizing it was over. At least for tonight, I had no idea if it were often this intense for the him. My entire body was shaking almost to seizure as I dripped blood on the floor. It took all the will power I had remaining to get up and carry the boy farther away. In the short distance from that room to where his father had been sleeping, I became so weak that I almost fainted upon reaching him. Still I am unsure as to whether my inability to explain what had happened was the result of my now diminished state or that I myself had not been able to accept the facts enough at the time to express them. However, I was able to provide a brief account of what had just occurred. After laying the boy down where the father was sleeping, I took the father to the room which was then empty and quiet as it should have been. His disbelief and astonishment upon viewing the video was more than a relief to me, as I was unsure of my own sanity at the time.

Never had the boy or the parents mentioned anything near as extreme as what happened that night, so I never again sought to study the boy for fear of making things worse for him. I do admit that my own cowardice also played a part in my decision to cut off contact.

My reputation was lost when I sought answers to the events of that night, which is what led to my current state of professional outcast. I lost close friends and colleagues due to my pursuit of answers to questions that seemed, even to me, to come from a delusional mind.

Now it seems that the shadows haunt me, they move with a purpose that I cannot—or will not understand. It is difficult to describe the visions that now haunt me and even more difficult to describe the state I am in. Are my new visions merely flashbacks to the night that shattered me, or are the shadows now punishing me for trying to interfere? No matter what the reality is, my new life is one of fear and little understanding. Now that I'm suffering from PTSD symptoms triggered by unusual events, I have become what I intended to study. I accepted that humanity knew so little of the universe, but I didn't really understand what that meant until that night. Something definitely happened that night that embodies the darkest nightmares of men, things which have yet no natural explanation.

Signed:

Philip Howard, PhD

Davin Creed *had taken a long hiatus from writing fiction, only to be pulled back in a few years ago through the enthusiasm and encouragement of his fiction writing brother.*